TAKE ME TO THE CABIN

A MOUNTAIN MAN ROMANCE

KACI ROSE

FIVE LITTLE ROSES PUBLISHING

COPYRIGHT

Book Cover By: **Wildheart Graphics**

Editing By: Debbe @ **On The Page, Author and PA Services**

Proofread By: Violet Rae

BLURB

DEDICATION

To all those who ever think of running off to the mountain and leaving everyday life behind, even just for a weekend.

CONTENTS

GET FREE BOOKS!

Do you like Military Men? Best friends brothers?
What about sweet, sexy, and addicting books?

If you join Kaci Rose's Newsletter you get these books free!

https://www.kacirose.com/free-books/

Now on to the story!

CHAPTER 1

JENNA

I'm shopping for my own place, and I can pick out anything I want.

If I want to decorate it like a disco ball, there's no one to tell me no, except well, maybe myself.

No one is going to tell me what to do, what to buy, what to wear. Not anymore.

These are such freeing thoughts, I keep saying them to myself over and over again.

I have a huge file on my computer of possible home decor ideas, with so much freedom to choose, I can't narrow it down.

I couldn't have picked a better place to be on my own. Whiskey River, Montana, is a small town with majestic mountain views. Walking down Main Street as I look to furnish my cabin, I'm surrounded by the breathtaking Montana mountains.

This is the most beautiful small town that no one has ever heard of. It's the type of town people move to and never leave. And it will be the perfect place for me to put down roots for the family I want to build.

Most of the shops and restaurants are mom-and-pop owned. All up and down Main Street and throughout downtown are benches so people can sit and take in the mountain views. It's easy to get lost in them and ignore everything else.

When I finally tear my eyes away from the mountain, Whiskey River Local Retail is the shop in front of me. In the window is a sign that says they have some hand-crafted items. This is the type of furniture and decor I want for my home. Local items, one-of-a-kind, handmade things that you won't see everywhere.

Walking into the store, I find it's larger than I realized. There's a whole outdoor and camping section to my left, the handmade items to my right, and an entire furniture section toward the back of the store.

I mentally tick off the items I want. I'll need a dining room table, a living room, and a bedroom set. For a two-bedroom cabin, the dining room is pretty big. I want a large table to fill it because I have dreams of friends gathering around that table some-day soon.

But first, I have to make friends, which means opening up about my past, and I'm not quite ready for that.

Taking a deep breath, I remind myself to start with the table, and then I can slowly find the friends to fill it.

My life here is still too new, and I'm not done looking over my shoulder. But I'll get there. I know I will. Since I plan to make Whiskey River my home, I need to relax and take my time making friends.

As I get to the back of the store, I stop dead in my tracks. Four men are talking to another man behind the counter.

Four very large, rugged men. As if they sense me staring, they all turn to look at me, and that's when I see the blonde girl with them. Compared to them, she's small. When she peeks her head around one of the men, she offers me a smile. The man standing beside her pulls her closer to his side, and they resume their conversation. so I return my attention to the furniture.

A wooden slab coffee table catches my eye. It's as if someone sliced a large tree from top to bottom like a slice of bread, and polished it up to make this table. You can see all the different patterns of the wood. If it were a dining room table, it would be perfect for my place.

"It's beautiful, isn't it?" The man behind the counter appears beside me.

"Yeah. I wish you had one like it as a dining room table."

"Phoenix over there made it. He makes all the wood furniture for the store. Let me ask him." The man walks over to the group of men.

I check out the rest of the wood furniture in the shop. There are rocking chairs and small tables, and every piece looks unique.

One of the men from the group slowly walks up to me. His eyes are on me the whole time, but not in the creepy way that makes me uncomfortable like...

No. I'm not going there. This man's whiskey-colored eyes are warm, almost comforting. He's large and slightly awkward as if he's afraid to make the wrong move and knock something over.

"Jack said you were looking for a table?" His deep rumbly voice washes over me, giving me goosebumps. His voice is scratchy, his words unsure as if he doesn't enjoy talking to strangers. Who can blame him?

I clear my throat, hoping he hasn't caught me staring. "I love this coffee table and wondered if you could make anything like this in a dining room table size."

He stares at me like he's trying to learn everything about me with one look, but his gaze doesn't make me uncomfortable. It has the opposite effect, putting me at ease. When he doesn't answer me right away, I begin to wonder if he heard my question.

Of course, this is the moment my phone rings. I tense because there are only three people who would call me. It's too late now, but I make a mental note to head into the city to get my phone changed.

Glancing at the screen, I see the call is from my mom. I send it to voicemail and look back up at the man in front of me.

He runs his hand through his deep brown hair with its enticing curl. "I'm working on one for a customer now." He pauses, and I think he's done when he speaks again. "You're welcome to come to my workshop to check it out, and see if it's what you are looking for."

Why does the thought of spending time with him excite me? It shouldn't because I don't know him. Shouldn't I be experiencing "stranger danger" rather than excitement?

"I'd like that," I hear myself saying.

My phone rings again. This time it's my dad. I send him to voicemail, too, something I've never done in my life. I'm surprised they gave me two entire weeks before they tried to find me.

"Sorry about that," I say, hoping he doesn't think I'm rude.

His eyes bore into mine. "No worries. I'm Phoenix."

"I'm Jenna. You might already know this, but I'm new to town." I feel the need to add the last part.

He nods and then turns to go to the counter.

"Okay, then," I mutter under my breath.

I start browsing the wall of home décor items, and a moment later, Phoenix is back at my side, thrusting a piece of paper at me.

"That's my shop and how to get there," he says.

I take the piece of paper, which contains not only an address, but also directions.

"When?" I ask.

"Tomorrow?"

"That works. Lunchtime?"

He nods, and his eyes lock with mine once again, keeping me frozen in place. I can't move or speak. All I can do is stare into those whiskey-colored eyes, knowing I'll be seeing them in my dreams tonight.

Hell, this man will fill my dreams for weeks to come. They don't make them this big, muscular, or sexy where I come from. If this is what men in Montana look like, I have no reason ever to leave.

When he finally turns and walks back to his friends, I instantly miss his eyes on me. It's an unfamiliar feeling.

After picking up decorations for the house, I go to pay for them. While the four guys watch my every move, the blonde woman smiles at me again. She seems friendly, even if the guy she's attached to looks like he could snap a car in half without breaking a sweat.

"Did you find everything you needed?" the man behind the counter asks.

"Mostly. I'm looking to furnish my new place."

"Well, whatever you can't find here, you can find in Helena, which is about an hour from here. It makes a good day trip into the city. Of course, I'm always happy to place an order for you," he tells me, ringing up my items.

"I'm sure I'll be taking you up on that," I reply as I pay him.

"What do you do for work?"

"I'm a photographer."

"What brings to our small town? I can't imagine there will be much work for you here."

"My most popular photos are from this area. When I was ready to start over, this is where I wanted to be."

"Well, let me know if you need any help." He hands me my bag and gives me a friendly smile.

I turn to the men, who are still staring at me. Offering them a shy smile, I head for the door.

Back on Main Street, I take a deep breath. My nerves are on edge, and not because I'm scared like I should be. I'm excited for tomorrow.

Maybe I should spend the afternoon taking photos with my camera and try to relax. I'm supposed to be starting over and focusing on myself, not getting excited over some guy.

No, I remind myself. I'm excited to go see the table and start decorating my home. That has to be it.

CHAPTER 2

PHOENIX

I can't believe I invited her to my place. I don't invite people to my place. Hell, other than Axel, Cash, and Bennett, I haven't had anyone out to my place, ever.

When I saw Jenna, a jolt went through me. I instantly felt comfortable with her, even more so than with the guys.

How is that possible?

Though, it was more than being comfortable with her. Her body tensed when her phone rang, and I had this overwhelming need to protect her. Whoever was calling, it was clear she didn't want to hear from them, and they called twice before taking the hint.

Inviting her to my place was as much a reason to check on her and make sure she's okay as it was for her to see the table. That's what I keep telling myself because I'm not sure how else to describe my feelings.

The guys were staring at me as Jenna left the store, and Emilie, Axel's wife, smiled like she knew some big secret. I pulled her aside to talk to her because I have zero experience with women, and Emelie explained that Jenna coming out to my place is a good sign. She wouldn't have agreed if she didn't feel secure and safe. Maybe she's attracted to me? The problem is, I don't know how I feel about her.

I wish I had more experience to draw on. My date to prom stood me up because someone better came along. My first kiss was a dare, and I haven't had one since. To say making friends didn't come easy to me growing up is an understatement. Axel, Bennett, and Cash are about it. And Jack, the guy who runs the store we sell our stuff from. We give each other space up here on the mountain.

Jenna will be here any time now, and I've already memorized the food and drinks I have to offer her. In preparation for her arrival, I've cleaned up my workshop, swept up all the sawdust, put my tools away, and moved all the scrap pieces of wood. I don't want any chance of her getting hurt while she's here.

When I'm working on a project, I get absorbed in it and it can get messy. Only when I've finished the project I'm working on do I clean up my workspace.

Normally woodworking is calming and I lose myself in it, but as I wait on Jenna, I can't even think about working on my current project. It's a long wooden slab dining room table like the one Jenna is looking for. I'm also making some chairs to go with the table. It's for a hotel a few towns over. They're updating their suites and wanted them furnished with local furniture. I don't mind because the contract pays well.

I'm beginning to think Jenna might not be coming when the telltale sound of a car engine fills the air. My driveway is long and winds up from the main road, so I have a few minutes before she gets here. I grab some sandpaper and work on the chair I should've been working on all morning.

Her car stops in front of my workshop, which is separate from the main house. I watch her as she gets out of the car. Like yesterday, she's wearing skintight jeans that show off her curves, but her shirt is looser, showing a hint of cleavage. Her light brown hair is pulled into some fancy side braid and the emerald-green eyes that captivated me yesterday are sparkling as she smiles.

That smile falters when she sees me and my heart sinks. Is she regretting coming out here? I can't blame her as it's not for everyone. Her eyes travel over my body and her cheeks turn pink. I suddenly remember I'm not wearing a shirt. I removed it earlier, and now I'm sweaty and covered in sawdust.

Despite all that, she walks toward me. "I love it out here. It's so quiet and the drive was beautiful," she says, pausing at the door of the workshop. It's a large rolling garage door that lets in tons of light and makes moving large furniture in and out of the building easy.

"It's quiet because there are no people. I don't like people," I tell her honestly.

This earns me a small smile. As uncomfortable as I am, if my honesty earns me those smiles, I'll keep it up.

She takes a few hesitant steps forward and looks at the table in the middle of the large workspace. "May I?"

I nod, and she steps closer, running her hand over the top of the table as she walks the length of it before looking up at me. Giving me one of those small, mysterious smiles, she turns to look out the side of the building, which has another large rolling door, although this one looks out over my cabin.

"What a beautiful cabin. It must be peaceful out here."

While I don't know a lot about women, even I can recognize small talk. Is she nervous like I am? I can't imagine a beautiful girl like Jenna being nervous around anyone.

"It's very peaceful. I built the cabin myself when I first moved here," I tell her, slowly making my way over to the other end of the workshop where she's standing.

I'm proud of my cabin because I didn't think I could do it or survive out here. It's proof that I'm right where I need to be, where I belong.

She looks at me, her eyes wide with shock. "You built that cabin?"

"I did. I bought three hundred acres here on the mountain, and that cabin was the first thing I built. It's what got me into my love of woodworking."

"Why all the way out here?"

This is a subject I'm not ready to get into. If I were with the guys and didn't want to talk about something, I would just give them a pointed stare, and they would know to back off. Something tells me that approach would scare Jenna, and that's the last thing I want to do. But I don't want to lie to her either, so I figure just being vague might be the best option.

"I like being self-sufficient out here. I grow all the trees I need for my woodworking, and I replant what I take. As you pointed out, there's plenty of peace and quiet." I shrug my shoulders, not sure what else to say.

"What do you mean by being self-sufficient out here?"

"I hunt and fish for my food, growing what I can. I don't waste anything. I rarely shop in town, and I use the money from my wood-working to buy what I need."

I can see her mind working. She's full of questions I don't want to answer right now, so I switch the topic to her.

"What brings you to town?"

· · · ● ●· ● ● · ·

Jenna

Wow. Phoenix with his shirt off is like looking at a god. Perfectly sculpted abs that glisten in the sunlight. Even sweaty, he looks like something out of a well-staged magazine ad. I've read in romance novels how a sight like that turns the heroine on, but I've never experienced anything like it until today.

It's like my body is calling out to him, telling me he's the one to mate with, to protect me, to save me. I have no doubt I'd be safe in those powerful arms, but that doesn't mean he wants anything to do with my drama. He said it himself. He's out here because he doesn't like people, and my drama would only bring people he doesn't want into his life.

When Phoenix told me he lives out here and is self-sufficient, I wanted to know more. I'm curious how he does it, and want all the details behind it. A self-sufficient life here in the Montana mountains appeals to me more than I can admit out loud. The problem is, I'd have no idea where to start.

It's obvious Phoenix is uncomfortable talking about himself. He's a little awkward, and

I'm guessing that's from living out here, not having to deal with social interactions every day. It's one of the things I like about him. He's real and not hardened by society on how to feel or act.

"I'm a landscape and nature photographer. The photos I took out here a few years ago are my best sellers. When I was asked to do a photo book on the area, I agreed. I knew even then I felt at home, so I decided to come live here."

"What kind of book?" he asks as he turns and walks to the other side of his workshop, putting the large table between us.

I don't answer right away, watching him and enjoying the way his body moves as he opens a small cooler.

"Turkey sandwich?" he asks, holding up a small paper bag.

"That sounds delicious."

Stepping back into the workshop, I take the bag from him, and we settle on one of his workbenches to eat. I take the first bite. For someone who's self-sufficient out in the mountains, this is one of the best sandwiches I've had in a very long time.

"This sandwich is really good."

He watches me for a moment as he takes another bite of his sandwich. I get the feeling he's thinking about his words before he speaks, something I wish more people did. Heck, it's something I wish I did more of myself.

"I grow the vegetables and I shot the turkey myself. Fresh ingredients make the difference," he says slowly like he's thinking about each word.

After a few more bites, he sits in silence, and I decide to answer his question from earlier. "The photo book I'm doing is about life in western Montana. The book has different sections, including small towns, way of life, natural scenery, and a small section on Yellowstone. A short description will accompany each photograph."

"Do you submit it to a publisher?"

"No, I already have a publisher. I'm submitting the photos with the descriptions, and they're doing the layout and other information. I'm not a writer, so they're working with someone to turn it into a story with my information and photos. I like this publisher because they're lenient with their deadlines. I have a year to do the book but I'm sure as we get closer to the deadline it won't seem like nearly enough time."

He doesn't smile, but one side of his mouth quirks up in what would be a cocky grin on anyone else. On him, it looks more like a shy smile. It's as if he doesn't know how to react to my statement.

"That sandwich was really good. Thank you for lunch. I wasn't expecting you to feed me while I was out here."

He shrugs, looking at the tools on his workbench before he answers. "It's a long drive back into town. Better to eat now."

Turning away, I look at the table to hide my smile. He doesn't talk much, but I find the little that he does say extremely interesting. He reveals more than he realizes.

As I look over the table, I say, "This table is too small for my dining room."

He hesitates, so I offer him another small smile to encourage him to talk, which seems to be what he needs. "I can come out and measure your space and custom make the table for you."

"Really? That would be great." I'm not sure if it's great because he can custom make the table for my space, or great because I'll get to see him again.

"I'll be done with this one in about two weeks and then I can start on yours."

We talk for a moment about the price, which seems to make him uncomfortable, so I agree to wait until he knows the specs to give me a solid bid.

"I was wondering." I hesitate because I sense he's going to tell me to fuck off in a nice way.

"Yeah?" He shifts on his feet and shoves his hands into his pockets.

"Feel free to tell me no. There would be no hard feelings. But I wondered if I could come back and talk to you for my book?"

He looks uncomfortable. I can't blame him because he moved out here to get away from everybody. Suddenly having someone wanting to talk to him about his way of life must be disconcerting. Yet, I'm hoping that he'll say yes. I'm willing to bet he knows these mountains better than anyone and can point me in the right direction for some great places to photograph. If nothing else, I'll get to spend a little more time with him.

But if he says no, I have to be okay with that. At least I'll see him in a few weeks when he comes out to measure the space for my dining room table. Maybe by then, he'll have warmed up to the idea.

He rubs the back of his neck and stares at his feet before glancing up at me. "I guess that would be okay."

I can't stop the big smile that takes over my face."When works for you? My schedule is pretty open."

"Tomorrow morning? I'll be working on this table, and I can talk and work at the same time."

"Tomorrow morning is perfect. See you then."

CHAPTER 3

PHOENIX

Jenna is coming back out today to talk to me about her book. I looked online last night, and her photos are good. I can see why the ones she took in this area are her best sellers. They're my favorites, too.

I spent hours flipping through the photos, mesmerized by her ability to find different angles of some popular locations in places like Yellowstone. I'm not sure what she wants to know about me, but I'm happy to help her because I can't wait to see what she does with this book.

I couldn't sleep last night, knowing she was coming today, so I've been up since dawn working on the chairs. I have three more before this order is complete, and so long as I stay on track, they'll be done early. That means that I can start on Jenna's table sooner, which will give me more time to spend with her.

When the sound of her car making its way up my driveway fills the silence, I glance at the clock. It's just after 8:00 a.m., which means I'll get to spend a good part of the day with her. As nervous as that makes me, I'm also excited.

I've never liked having people around me while I work, but it's different with Jenna. Maybe I can figure out why after spending some time with her today.

When she steps out of the car, she takes my breath away. She's dressed in jeans, a T-shirt with a sweater, and boots. Her attire is casual and she's not wearing much makeup, but she looks even more beautiful than when she was dressed up yesterday.

"You can sit there." I nod to the chair I placed in the corner of the workshop so she would be safely out of the way as I work.

Nodding, she takes a seat and watches me work on the chair I'm finishing up. I get lost in my task as I usually do, and when she speaks, it startles me.

"You're good at what you do."

My face heats, and I keep my gaze on the chair. "It's redundant work when you have to do twelve chairs all the same."

"What makes your stuff beautiful is that you pay attention to detail."

To change the subject, I ask, "What questions do you have in your notebook?"

Holding up her notebook, she gives me an enticing smile and, thankfully, lets me off the hook. "Is it common for the people out here to be self-sufficient like you?"

I stop and think because, while I don't want to betray my friend's privacy, I want to answer her questions the best I can. "It's not common, but it's not unheard of either. Those that work in town tend to live there, and they're not as self-sufficient as I am. But the winters out here are rough, so they stock up and know how to get by when they can't leave their house for any length of time."

"But they're not self-sufficient in the way you are living out here."

"No. You saw my friends at the shop. They're self-sufficient like I am, and there are others out here in the mountains. We own our plot of land and live off of it. But not all of us are friendly. When I first moved here, I was looking for property and stumbled on a cabin owned by a man who wanted nothing to do with anyone. He never goes into town, and he lives completely off-grid, as your city folks call it."

She scribbles down notes while I continue to work, waiting for her to ask the next question.

"How off-grid are you and your friends?"

"My friends are even more off-grid than I am. The four of us have a radio to check in if we need anything. Since I go into town more often than they do, I'll pick up supplies and take them to their homes. I have satellite internet at the cabin, but I don't use it much. The reception is pretty spotty, but I can use it to make emergency calls."

Jenna scribbles down some notes before checking her phone. "I don't have service out here. The Wi-Fi doesn't come out to the workshop?"

"If I wanted service here, I could get it. But I moved here to get away from people and electronics. Since the workshop is my sanctuary, I don't want anybody interfering with that. The only exception is the radio in case the guys need to get hold of me." I nod toward the radio on my workbench. I also have one in the house, but I don't need to go into too much detail with her.

"So, you spend all the warmer months preparing for winter?"

With that question, I go into all the details of winter prep. I tell her about the hunting and fishing, how I prepare the meat to be stored, and what sort of creature comforts I have compared to when I lived in town.

Although Jenna asks about my life before I moved out here, I shut those questions down as it's not something I'm willing to talk about. Thankfully, she drops it.

We talk more about what winters are like in these mountains and how I learned how to take care of myself out here.

Outside of being stood up for prom in high school, I have no experience with women, so I'm not sure if Jenna is flirting with me or not. She's smiling a lot, that soft smile I love. Sometimes when she says something, and I don't get what she means, her cheeks flush pink. A flush I find incredibly sexy.

When she's embarrassed, she looks down at her notebook and tucks her hair behind her ear. At one point, she walks over to look at what I'm doing with the chair, and her shoulder brushes mine. Though she apologizes, she doesn't move away. When her eyes land on my lips and her tongue darts out to lick hers, I've never wanted to kiss anyone more in my whole life.

But she's here to get some information for her book. There's no way she sees me like that. After a moment, I go back to working on the chair, and she sits back down to scribble in her notebook. She doesn't ask me any questions for a while, just watches me work. I thought I'd be uncomfortable with her in my workspace, but it's comforting to have her here.

"I like how there's no phone reception or Wi-Fi in your workshop. It can be such a distraction, and I'm sure I'd get so much more done if I could find a place like this to work," she says quietly, almost as if talking to herself.

Words spill from my mouth before I can think, shocking me. "You're more than welcome to come back tomorrow. Bring your stuff to get some work done, and we can talk some more if you have any other questions."

Not wanting her to see how hopeful I am that she'll take me up on my offer, I look down at what I'm working on. If she says no, I don't want her to see the disappointment I won't be able to hide.

"If you're sure, I'd like to take you up on that," she says.

"I'm sure."

When I turn to look at her, she offers me another one of her killer smiles before packing up her stuff. She says her goodbyes and promises to be back tomorrow at the same time.

After watching her car drive away, I try to get back to work, but it doesn't feel the same now she's gone. It's hard to concentrate on the intricate details when Jenna's smile invades my thoughts.

Deciding to switch gears, I load my truck with some lumber to take over to Axel's place, who's building a small addition to his home. The upside to taking the lumber is his wife Emelie might have some insights about Jenna. Axel is the first of us to get married, and Emelie has taken the rest of us under her wing. She's always baking for us and offering advice, so I know she'll be happy to sit down and talk to me if I get up the guts to say what's on my mind.

Parking as far up Axel's drive as I can, I walk the rest of the way to his cabin. Since he isn't expecting me, the first thing I see when he opens the door is the shotgun and then him.

It doesn't even surprise me. Now that he's married, he's very protective—not that he hasn't always been cautious about safe-guarding his land.

"If you'd let me know you were coming, I wouldn't have greeted you with a shotgun," Axel grunts.

I shake my head. "You don't scare me. I brought some of the lumber you wanted. If you hook up the four-wheelers with the trailers, I can help you bring it up to the house."

He nods, setting the rifle down.

"Please tell me you'll stay for dinner, Phoenix," Emelie calls from inside the house.

"Of course, I'll stay."

Axel and I hook up the trailers to the four-wheelers and head down to my truck.

"What's on your mind?" he asks as we un-load the lumber from my truck.

"Jenna."

"The girl from the shop?"

"Yeah. She was at my place again today, and she's coming out tomorrow, too. I find her hard to read."

"Women, in general, are hard to read. Talk to Emelie about it. You know she'll be happy to point you in the right direction because she's ready to have more females on the mountain," Axel smirks.

"I don't know if it's going that far, but I'm at ease around her, so that's something."

After unloading the lumber, Axel leans against my truck and crosses his arms, staring at me. He's bigger than me, but only by a few inches in height. Muscle-wise we're on an even playing field, but he has a way of making me feel intimidated.

"From the moment my eyes locked with Emilie's on that riverbank, I knew she was mine. Who would think I'd be grateful for a storm flooding out the road so she couldn't leave? The thought of her going tore out my heart, and that was before I understood my feelings for her. I was comfortable around her, and I liked having her in my space."

"I know what you mean. There was something there when I saw Jenna at the shop the other day. I'm comfortable with her in my space. And yeah, I'm excited for her to come back tomorrow. Even though she just moved to town, I don't have the feeling that she's going to leave."

We don't say anything else. Axel just nods, and we drive the four-wheelers back up to his cabin, unloading the lumber at the back where he plans to add to the main living area.

Dinner, as always, is delicious. We catch up, making plans for me to help with the building of the cabin and go hunting together. Then the conversation turns to plans for the upcoming winter and all the things required to be self-sufficient up here on the mountain.

Emelie is still learning and asks a lot of questions, and it's her that walks me outside as I get ready to leave. I know Axel has told her about our conversation as they tell each other everything, so I don't have to repeat what I told him earlier.

"If she's making plans to come back out to your workshop in the middle of nowhere, it's a good sign. The best thing you can do is be yourself. If she didn't like being around you, she wouldn't spend more time with you. One of the things you'll have to do is make her understand this way of life. If it's not for her, you want to find out sooner rather than later. And don't tell her, show her."

With that, Emilie hugs me and sends me on my way with a pie and a lot to think about.

Chapter 4

Jenna

I'm driving up the mountain to spend another day with Phoenix, and I can't help but wonder what it would be like if this were my drive home. The more he talks about the self-sufficient life he lives out here, the more I want something like it.

More than anything, I enjoyed hanging out with Phoenix. He's not like the guys I grew up with or dated in the past. He's awkward and a bit raw with his feelings and emotions.

I grew up where everything was fake. You never knew who liked you for you or for what you could do for them. In most cases, it was the latter. So, to me, raw emotions are like a breath of fresh air.

Today, I brought my camera. I don't know if Phoenix will let me take any photos, but I hope I can convince him. I pull up to his workshop where he has both large garage doors open, and he stops and smiles when he sees me.

It's a genuine smile, not forced. I can't remember the last time someone smiled at me the way Phoenix is smiling at me. It makes my heart skip a beat and floods my stomach with new sensations.

I park my car and gather my stuff, feeling his eyes on me the whole time, and when I turn to open my car door, he's right there holding it open for me. Such a gentleman.

"I set up a little table for you off to the side, but we can move anything around that you need." He takes my computer bag from me, and we make our way into the workshop.

"But I don't want to be in the way, and I don't want you to have to rearrange your workshop. Don't worry about me. I can fit in wherever there's room," I tell him as I take in the small table and chair in the corner he's cleared for me.

"You aren't in the way, I promise. I wanted to make sure you were comfortable." He sets my computer bag on the table and steps back to allow me to get situated.

I can see out both large garage doors from this corner to the cabin beyond. Plus, I have the perfect view of him working. "Thank you. This is perfect. I brought my camera because I was hoping you'd let me take some pictures while you're working. I don't have to include your face if you don't want me to."

He seems uncomfortable with the idea and doesn't answer right away. When he shifts on his feet, I'm sure he's going to say no. "None of my face or any identifying places like my cabin or the truck. And if you plan to use them, I'd like to have approval first."

I'd planned to get his okay before using any of the photos I took of him or his property, but he's smart to double-check. Once again, I wonder about his background before he came to the mountain. Maybe someday, he'll share it with me.

"Of course, and if at any point you're uncomfortable or I get in the way, please tell me." Sitting down at the table, I pull out my computer, planning to start with the photo editing I've been putting off.

He nods, turning to get back to work.

I edit photos over the next hour, glancing up often to watch him and finding his eyes already on me. He smiles shyly at me when I catch him and gets back to work. We work in comfortable silence for a while until Phoenix speaks again.

"What photos are you editing?" He nods towards my computer.

"On my way up here, I drove through Yellowstone, and I took my time taking lots of photos. I sort through them to see what I might use in my book. Then I edit them to put on stock photo sites, which can earn me decent money from people purchasing them."

I expect some questions about what a stock photo site is, but he just nods and smiles. I wonder if he knows or if he's just not interested.

I can't take my eyes off his muscular body as he sands down the edges of a chair. Pulling out my camera, I focus on his hands working on the wood and snap a few photos. When he hears the click of the camera, he stops and looks at me.

"Come take a look." I stand up and pull the photos up on the camera's screen. All you can see is the edge of the chair in his hands as he works on it.

"I don't see how that photo is of any interest." He shakes his head and turns back to the chair.

"This photo embodies you. It's woodworking, but it shows how you're self-sufficient in making things as simple as a chair. A picture can say a thousand words, and even the simplest picture can tell a story. Anyway, this picture is just for me." When he looks up at me, I give him a wink and sit back down in my chair.

While I know I shouldn't be flirting with him, I can't help myself. Being around this big, rough mountain man makes me feel feminine. He brings out a different side of me, and I feel safe with him. I love watching his reaction to me, almost like he isn't sure how to respond to my small-talk.

As he gets back to work, I position my camera to take a few more photos. Watching him through my camera lens and seeing his attention to detail gives me a whole new appreciation for his work. His hands are rough, calloused, and tell a story all of their own.

I snap a few photos of him for myself that no one else will see, like when he wipes his hands on his jeans as he takes a closer look at the chair. After taking a few more photos, I set the camera down and get back to work editing photos.

"Are you hungry? I made some sandwiches-." His voice breaks through my editing fog.

"You didn't have to do that, but I am hungry. If you allow me to come back and work here again, I'll supply lunch next time."

"You're welcome back anytime, but you don't have to supply lunch. I'm happy to do it."

"But if I make lunch, I can include my favorite fudge chocolate cookies. They're pretty much the only thing I can bake well."

He laughs as he pulls our sandwiches from the cooler and brings mine over to me. Leaning against the workbench closest to me, we stop and eat.

"So, what do you do when you have down-time up here on the mountain?"

"I don't really have downtime." He shrugs like it's no big deal and takes another bite of a sandwich.

"Even in the winter?"

"When we get snowed in, I'll generally have some wood in the house to make smaller things. I like to read. Jack will order books by the box because he loves to read, too, and when he's done, he'll pass them on to the guys and me."

"What do you like to read?"

"Mystery and suspense, mostly."

His conversation is short and right to the point, but he's not unwilling to answer questions. We chat while we finish our lunch, saving subjects about our pasts, our families, or what brought us to Whiskey River for another time.

After lunch, we both get working again, and when Phoenix finishes the chair, I start to put my stuff away and get ready to head out. I've gotten more work done today than I have since I moved here.

Getting up to stretch my legs, I step outside with my camera to look around the workshop and the cabin. Phoenix seems so engrossed in what he's working on that I don't think he realizes I'm no longer in the workshop anymore.

When I look at the woods bordering the driveway, a bright blue shape in a tree catches my attention. I zoom in with my camera, seeing a Mountain Bluebird, and snap some pictures.

Something startles it, and it flies off. I lower the camera, and further into the woods, I spot a wolf with four little pups at her feet.

Even though the mama wolf is standing there watching me, I'm far enough away to not be a threat. I lift my camera and zoom in to get some photos of the pups playing.

Two of them look like they're trying to bite each other, and it's the cutest thing I've ever seen. Getting some photos of mama wolf watching over them as they play is making for some fantastic photos.

I get so lost in snapping pictures, I don't hear anyone coming up behind me. When an arm wraps around my waist and pulls me against a hard chest, I let out a squeal of surprise, and the wolves go running.

Looking over my shoulder, I find Phoenix with an angry look on his face. It's a little overpowering, but then I realize he's not wearing a shirt. His bare chest pressed to my back is turning me on, and the anger on his face isn't cooling me off one bit.

He pulls me back to the workshop before letting me go. Even though I know he's mad, just having his arm around me is a turn-on and confusing as hell. He's angry, but it's making me hot. I've never experienced that before, and I don't know what to make of it.

"What the hell were you thinking?" he demands once we reach the workshop.

"What? I was just taking photos," I say as I start flipping through the photos on my camera.

"This isn't the zoo. Those are wild animals. One wrong move and that wolf would have attacked you to protect those pups. She would have torn you to shreds!" he yells.

I've never heard this man raise his voice. Hell, most of the time, I struggle to hear him. Looking up at him, I realize he's serious about this.

"But I didn't look for them. I was taking photos of a bird and saw the wolves. I was plenty far away. I know animal safety, and I was just as safe as you would've been walking to your cabin."

"No more wandering off. I'm not having you get hurt on my watch. You stay in the workshop. It's too dangerous out there." Some of the fight has left him, and I think we both realize we need some space.

After staring at each other for a while, he speaks again, back to his calm self. "I should have this chair finished over the weekend. The guys and I are meeting at the shop on Monday. If you want to meet us there around one, I can come out and measure the space to get started on your table."

At least he still wants to spend time with me. Maybe things will be different in a few days.

"I'll be there."

Leaving knowing that I'll see him again in just a few short days has me feeling lighter than I have since I left Denver. But I should have known my past will always come back to haunt me.

CHAPTER 5

PHOENIX

Today, I'm loading up the items I'm taking into the shop. It's mostly smaller home decor stuff. I keep looking over at the corner with the table and chair I set up for Jenna. I was going to take them into the shop today, but they already feel like they're hers like that's her spot, and I can't bring myself to remove them.

I want her to have a place when she comes here. I hope she continues to visit because I enjoyed having her in my space. Even if I didn't understand her fascination with taking pictures of me while I work.

As I head into town, I get more and more excited about seeing her in just a few short hours. The guys and I are meeting at the shop at noon, which should give us plenty of time to catch up and unload our stuff for Jack before she shows up.

When I get to the shop, I find Axel and Bennett's trucks at the back, but Cash isn't here yet. I park my truck, grab a box, and go in the back door.

There are boxes already sitting on the table Jack has set up in the back room for us so I'm assuming that Axel and Bennett are done unloading. Going back to my truck, I grab the last two boxes and set them on the table.

A quick peek in the other boxes shows Axel brought in a bunch of his homemade jerky and some of his hand-carved knives. He carves these intricate mountain scenes on knife handles. If Jenna thinks I'm great at the detail, she should see his stuff.

Axel focuses more on hunting equipment--bows and arrows, in particular. Cash brings in items made from the furs of the animals he catches.

Once I have my boxes unloaded, I go into the store and find them chatting with Jack by the register.

Emelie comes bouncing up to me with a huge smile on her face. "I've been waiting for you to get here. You have to tell me how it was with Jenna at the workshop, and I want all the details."

She wraps her arm in mine, walking me back to the group. Axel watches her but doesn't say anything. He always has his eyes on her, making sure she's safe while allowing her to be herself.

"When Cash gets here, so I don't have to repeat myself," I reply.

The smile falls from her face and her shoulders sag a little, but Axel pulls her into his side and her smile returns.

Watching the two of them together gives me hope I might be able to find that, to find what my parents had. It didn't seem possible up here on the mountain until I saw how Axel and Emelie found each other.

"I thought he'd be here by now. He's usually one of the first to arrive," Jack says.

None of us gets a chance to respond as Cash walks through the door. He looks tired and worn out, and while we won't pry, I know Emelie will.

"Cash, is everything okay?" Emelie rushes to his side.

"My brother is getting sicker, and declining fast. Now he's delusional and the doctor only gave him a month to live. In order to get here today, I had to wait until he was asleep from the sleeping medication so I could slip out."

Cash told us his brother had been sick for a while. When he finally got a doctor to look at him, they found a brain tumor. He refused treatment because he doesn't trust the government or doctors. From the time Cash was six, his brother has raised him and he knows no other life than here on the mountain.

"What can we do?" I ask him.

He shakes his head. "Over the next few weeks, I might need you to come to get my stuff for the shop. He's sleeping now, but I don't want to leave him again because he's going downhill fast."

"You got it. Let me know when you have things to pick up," I tell him.

This is the reason I insisted on the radio for these guys, so they had a way to ask for help when needed. Now, I'm even more relieved that I thought about it and I'm sure Cash is, too.

Of all the guys, I'm the one who will do extra town runs for them. I don't mind people as much as they do. Axel moved to the mountains because his size tended to scare people and he got tired of all the stares—at least until he met Emelie.

Cash only comes to town to drop off items here at the store. Since their parents died, his brother has handled everything else.

As for Bennett, none of us know much of his back story, other than he was in the military and doesn't like to be around people.

These men would be there to help me with anything I needed at the drop of a hat–and they have in the past–so I have no problem doing the same for them.

"I'll put together some freezer meals that you can warm up, so food is one less thing you have to worry about," Emelie says.

"I can take your payments to the bank and deposit them," Jack says. "Then Phoenix can bring you the receipts."

"Thank you," Cash says, but I know he's uncomfortable asking for help. We all are, but we do it when we need it.

"Tell me what else is going on. I could use some good news," he says, looking at me.

"Phoenix was going to tell us about his date with Jenna!" Emelie says excitedly.

"It wasn't a date," I grumble, but something in my heart flutters.

Was it a date? We had lunch, we worked to-gether and talked. I'm pretty sure she flirt-ed, but there was no kiss. I'm pretty sure it's not a date if it doesn't end in a kiss.

"If she came out to your place to spend time with you, it was a date," Emelie smirks.

"She came out to work because there was no phone service and no distractions," I cor-rect her, but that only earns me an eye roll.

"Really? She could have parked at any mountain overlook outside of town, but she wanted to be around you," Emilie says.

Switching gears, I tell them she's coming by in a bit so I can follow her to her place and measure for the table she wants.

"If she makes plans to see you again, no matter if it's coming to your place or meet-ing you in town, she's interested," Emelie says, and the guys all nod their heads.

"Interested in having me build her table."

"It's more than that, and you know it," Emile says sternly.

"I guess we'll see."

"If things go well at her place, invite her out to do something you enjoy but not work-related. If she accepts, you'll have your answer," Emelie says with a twinkle in her eye.

We chat for a little longer with Jack before the bell over the door rings, and I turn to see Jenna walking in hesitantly.

Like every time I see her, she takes my breath away. Even in everyday clothes, she's the most stunning woman I've ever seen. When her eyes land on mine, she smiles, and with that simple smile, my nerves evaporate.

She walks over to the group, and I take a few steps toward her, deciding I should make introductions. "Jenna, let me introduce you to the guys."

Jenna nods, looking around me. Placing my hand on her lower back, I guide her over to the group. That simple contact set my whole body on fire. Though I've felt like this before, it's something I want a lot more of.

"The guy behind the counter is Jack. You met him when you were here last time. And this is Bennett and Cash. Over there is Axel and his wife, Emelie. Everyone, this is Jenna."

"It's so nice to have another girl around. We'll have to do lunch and town one day-." Emelie walks over and wraps Jenna in a quick hug.

"I'd like that. I haven't had time to meet anyone in town yet," Jenna says.

Suddenly, I wish I could introduce her to everyone in town, but outside of the people currently in the shop, I don't know anyone.

"You ready?" I ask, and Jenna nods. "My truck's in the back, so I can follow you there," I tell her as we head towards the door after saying our goodbyes to everyone.

"I saw your truck when I pulled into the parking lot, so I parked near it. Hope that's okay."

"It's perfect as it allows me to walk you to your car."

Even though we walk the rest of the way in silence, it's comfortable and easy. Once I help Jenna into her car, I follow her back to her cabin.

Not far from the town, her place is secluded with no neighbors, and she has a pretty decent-sized yard surrounded by woods. After the leaves fall, I'm sure she'll have a beautiful mountain view.

"It's small, but it's all mine." She smiles as we go into her house.

I don't say anything but look around as we step inside. It's a true wood cabin with logwood walls, vaulted ceilings, and big windows to let in tons of natural light. There's a stone fireplace in the living room and some stone accents in the kitchen.

It's pretty empty inside. There are a few boxes in the living room but no couch or TV. There's one bar stool at the kitchen island, but no place to eat in the dining room. The only wall decor is what she bought at the shop the other day.

"When does the rest of your stuff get here?" I ask without thinking.

"This is the rest of my stuff. It's what I could fit in my car."

My mind starts racing about how I can help her furnish the house.

As if she can read me, she steps up and places her hand on my arm. "I have what I need and I'm enjoying slowly decorating my house. I don't want just anything. I want the perfect items. Besides, I haven't been spending much time here, anyway." She smiles as she looks me right in the eye, and I can't argue with her.

I open my mouth to ask her to spend some more time with me tomorrow, as Emelie suggested, but she removes her hand from my arm and clears her throat, taking a step back.

"This space over here is the dining room. I'd like a table to fill it and the chairs to go with it. The way I figure, if I build a large table, I'll have plenty of time to fill it with friends and maybe family later on." She shrugs her shoulders as she shows me the space beside the kitchen.

For a small cabin, it has a large dining room. I take my tape measure and the notepad I brought in from my truck and start making some notes.

"Would you like some iced tea?"

"That sounds good. I'm just going to measure the space," I tell her.

No sooner does Jenna set the two glasses of iced tea down on the kitchen island than there's a knock on the door. She looks a little startled but doesn't say anything as she makes her way to answer it. I keep taking my measurements, angling myself so I can keep an eye on Jenna.

She opens the door to a man dressed in a smart suit. The kind of man my parents used to do business with. Instantly, I'm on edge.

"Hey, baby. I missed you, and I couldn't wait to talk to see you again. Can we talk?" he asks in his smooth voice.

Of course, she's taken. I'm such an idiot. Why would she want anything to do with the mountain man who has zero experi-

ence with women when she's got a man like
that waiting on her?

CHAPTER 6

JENNA

What. The. Fuck?

What is Chad doing here?

How is Chad here?

How did he find me?

"No, I have company. I left for a reason," I grit out, trying not to cause a scene.

Chad knows exactly why I left. As I was leaving the church, I had a bridesmaid deliver a note to him. The text messages I got before ditching my phone and getting a new one confirmed they read it. It's been so peaceful since I got a new number.

"I just want to talk and figure out what happened. I know we can work this out." He tries to step inside, but I edge the door closed.

"You know what happened. Do not step foot on my property again." When I try to close the door, he stops me with his hand. - There's a sudden shift in him. He morphs from the pleasant boyfriend trying to calm me to an angry man I don't recognize.

"We lost every penny on that wedding. You *will* pay me back for it," he growls.

He thinks he's intimidating, and at one time, he was, but not anymore.

No, he's not one bit intimidating. I've seen guys like Axel and how gentle he is with Emelie but he'd still be able to snap Chad's neck with a flick of his wrist. The thought makes me smirk, which pisses off Chad even more. Win, win.

"Go talk to my parents seeing as you're all such good friends." I doubt my parents will pay him back, but it does fall on them to make things right. I can only imagine the stories they're spinning back home to save face in society.

"You will pay me back, or I'll make your life here a living hell."

"The last five years with you were a living hell, so do your worst. You won't get a dime from me." I slam the door this time and lock it, sagging in relief.

"You'll regret this!" Chad yells through the door.

The only thing I regret is letting it go as far as our wedding rehearsal before putting an end to it.

I want to cry, but then I remember Phoenix is here. He'll have seen and heard the whole thing from the dining room.

Shit. I can't seem to catch a damn break.

I have some explaining to do. I was hoping my past wouldn't catch up with me this fast—if at all—but I've never been that lucky. Things have been good with Phoenix-. Nothing too personal or deep, but I know he won't let this go.

No one in their right mind would let it go and continue to flirt with me unless they were only looking to get laid. Phoenix doesn't seem like that kind of guy. I hope he's not that kind of guy.

I walk back to the dining room to find him finishing up the measurements with an unreadable expression on his face.

"That was my ex... fiancé." There's the truth I was hoping to avoid when I moved here. But as my grandma always said, you can't run from your past, no matter how hard you try—and I'm trying pretty damn hard.

Phoenix studies me before turning and setting his stuff down on the kitchen island. While I don't know what's running through his mind, at least he isn't leaving.

When he turns to face me, the only way I can describe the look on his face is hopeful. He moves in front of me and takes my hands in his. "What happened?"

For the first time, I wish I had a couch in here. I don't want to have this conversation standing up, and sitting on my bed seems inappropriate.

Taking his hand, I walk over to the wall and sit down with my back against it. He sits facing me, still holding my hand.

"I left him the day of our wedding rehearsal. Packed up what I could fit in my car and left Denver without looking back. When we were at the rehearsal, I stood at the altar, and though I was looking at him, he was looking at everyone but me. Until that moment, it was like I'd been under a spell because suddenly, everything was crystal clear. The conversations, the way he acted." I shake my head, not wanting to go too far down that road.

"How did he act?" Phoenix asks softly, giving my hand a gentle squeeze.

"He was more interested in my parents, their company, and their money than me. As you heard, he was more anxious about me paying back the money he shelled out and lost by not getting married than he was about getting me back. On my way here, I spent a lot of time thinking and realized I loved the idea of being in love with him. I loved planning our wedding. I loved the life

I thought we'd have. I loved his family, but I didn't love *him*."

"That was a lot to happen all at once." His tone is soft but I can tell there's a lot going on in his head.

"I knew this is where I wanted to move. Without question, it's been a dream of mine to move here. The night I got into town, I stayed at the bed-and-breakfast, and the next day I went to the real estate office. Two days later, I found this place, and it just felt like home. I took what money I had from my grandparent's trust fund to buy it, and that was the last of the family money I used. Anyway, they cut me off, and before I got a new phone, they made that very clear."

Neither of us says a word as Phoenix takes it all in, but there's one more thing I want to add to make my point.

"After purchasing my cabin, I was able to get internet, which will be essential for my business. Then I pitched my book idea to the publisher that took my last book, and they called me the next day to make an offer on it. That's when I knew in my heart that this is where I'm meant to be. This is where I'm putting down roots, and why I'm taking my time making this into a home. I want it to be perfect. I can sell photos and give photography lessons to tourists in season to make money to pay my bills. I've received an advance for my book, which is a great help. I'm standing on my own two feet for the first time, and I've never felt more myself."

"What are your plans for when this book is done?"

"I have a year to figure that out, but I think I want to find some beautiful spots around here and offer photography lessons to tourists. They do it down in Jackson Hole, and it's incredibly popular, especially catching the sunrise on the mountains. This area is even more beautiful, so I'll continue to sell my photos, and if I'm smart, I can live off the income from those. I can always sell more books, or do family portraits and weddings. I'd rather fail and live in my car than go home." I shrug because the thought did cross my mind.

But as I sit there and stare into Phoenix's eyes, I'm sure there's more than one reason I belong here in Whiskey River.

· · · · ● · ● · · · ·

Phoenix

I hate thinking anybody has a claim on her, especially the guy at the door. I've always trusted my gut when it comes to people, and it's yet to steer me wrong. Right now, my gut says that guy is nothing but bad news.

I can't be mad at Jenna for not telling me about him because there are things in my past she doesn't know either. The plan has always been to get to know each other slowly, and that hasn't changed.

"I love it here in Montana. It's so peaceful, and I've never felt closer to nature," Jenna says, pausing to catch her breath. "And I like being at your workshop and watching you work. Being disconnected from the rest of the world is freeing, and I can see its appeal..."

Before I realize what I'm doing, I lean forward and cover her lips with mine just to get her to shut her brain off. Or, at least, I hope it does because that's what this kiss is doing to *my* brain. All I can think about is how soft her lips are and how she's melting into me.

While this isn't my first kiss, it's been a while. My last was a dare during my senior year of high school a decade ago. This is my first kiss that means something, but I don't want Jenna to know that.

Leaning forward, I cup her face in my hands before running them through her brown, silky hair. I'm finally getting to touch her, something I've been wanting to do since we met, so I take my time. I move slowly, exploring her plump lips, nibbling on them and pulling her closer, not that there's much space between us to begin with.

When she moans, I know I'm doing something right. Not wanting to jinx it, I pull away and rest my forehead on hers to catch my breath. My whole body is tingling with want—wanting her skin on mine, wanting so much more than just a kiss.

"I was not expecting that," Jenna says breathlessly.

I chuckle, not sure I can speak.

She reaches up and lightly traces a finger along my bottom lip.

"I liked it, too," I say, placing a soft kiss on her finger.

Emelie's words flash through my mind. Sitting here with Jenna smiling at me after that kiss, I know I want to explore whatever this is between us.

"Will you come to the cabin tomorrow? I want to show you one of my favorite places on the mountain."

"I would love that," Jenna says with a smile.

Leaning in, I place a soft, chaste kiss on her lips before standing up to get ready to go.

As I gather my stuff, I tell her, "Make sure to wear some hiking boots and comfortable clothing."

She stands and slowly walks me to the door. Even with the smile on her face, she looks a little stressed, and I hate to leave her. Knowing I'll see her tomorrow makes it easier.

I get in my truck, and the entire way home, all I can think about is that kiss. It's everything I hoped my first real kiss would be, and so much more. The moment I saw Jenna in the store, I knew she was special.

Being comfortable around her is a big thing for me because I'm not comfortable around just anyone. She's interested in me, and that's important because women in town generally see right through me. I don't even mind the drama of her ex.

But I don't like how stressed she looked when I was getting ready to leave. Was she anxious because I was leaving after everything that happened with her ex? Maybe she didn't want to be alone?

As I drive through town, I decide to follow my gut. I stop at the store, and when I walk in, Jack doesn't even hide his shock at seeing me.

"Phoenix? Is everything okay?" he asks, his voice full of concern.

Since I don't stop in unless it's my normal drop-off days, I'm not surprised he's concerned.

"I need a favor, and I can't give you too much information without betraying Jenna's trust," I tell him.

"Jenna is the girl who's interested in the table, right?"

Nodding, I get up the courage to ask my favor. Jack's always been great with the shop, but it wasn't until the issue with Emelie's ex-boyfriend and Axel being questioned by the police that Jack stepped up and showed he wanted to help us in any way that he could. It was also when he revealed to us that he was a lawyer before opening the shop here in Whiskey River.

"When you close up the shop, can you drive by Jenna's house and make sure everything looks okay. She had a visitor today who kind of shook her, and she looked a little stressed when I left. I just want to make sure everything is okay," I say as I scribble her address down on a piece of paper for Jack.

"Of course. I'll actually go one better and take her dinner so I have an excuse to check on her."

That's an even better idea. Knowing Jack will have eyes on her is a relief. I pull some money from my wallet and hand it to him.

"This should cover dinner for her and for you as a thank you for doing this. If anything is wrong, you know how to get hold of me."

Even though I have the internet at my cabin, I stay as disconnected as possible. It's satellite internet, and slower than most people are used to, but it allows me to have a satellite phone that I can reach Jack, and he can reach me as needed.

To stay in contact with Axel, Cash, and Bennett, we have a radio that we use to check on each other. We generally use it after big storms to make sure that we're all okay.

If they need something from town, they call and ask me to pick it up for them. Right now, with Axel working on his cabin, he'll radio me things he'd like Jack to order. I call it in so it's ready for him the next time he's in town.

With Jenna's safety taken care of, I get back in my truck and head to the cabin. This time, the only thing I can think about is the asshole demanding money from her. With her parents cutting her off, I know she won't be able to pay back the money anytime soon. And there's no telling how much he's trying to get from her.

The longer she has to deal with him, the longer he's going to be a sore spot, preventing us from moving forward with any type of relationship.

I could pay him off and not tell Jenna. Let her think he just disappeared into oblivion. But with a man like him, if I show him I have money to pay him off, he'll be constantly demanding money to stay out of her life.

This isn't how I wanted to start a relationship with her, but I'm sure as hell not going to let it stop me from going after what I want. Without a shadow of a doubt, I know Jenna is the one I want.

CHAPTER 7

JENNA

The last thing I wanted to do this morning was to get out of bed. It's probably a good thing I don't have a way to cancel on Phoenix because I probably would have stayed in and not left my nice warm covers. I kept thinking about how Axel safeguards Emelie and how much I want that. Last night I dreamt of a life out here with Phoenix and having him protect me like Axel does his wife.

By the time I'm driving out of town, I'm grateful I didn't cancel because the last place I want to be is at my cabin now my ex knows my address. Being on the mountain today with Phoenix sounds like the perfect getaway.

When Jack brought me dinner last night, he said it was courtesy of Phoenix, who wanted to make sure I was okay and had something to eat. I invited him in and we ate together and talked. He told me he's never seen Phoenix so protective of someone.

Jack also told me about his life before opening the store. How he was a lawyer and was forced to defend criminals who admitted they were guilty. The firm he worked for expected him to acquit them of whatever crime they were charged with. It wasn't long before he decided he couldn't, in clear conscience, keep doing it.

I asked Jack why he didn't just open up his own little practice. He told me he'd been thinking about it but he came here to Whiskey River on vacation and just never left. The store was up for sale, and on a whim, he bought it. He expanded it to what it is today, and he hasn't looked back.

Jack made a point to tell me that his license is still active if I were to need his services.

He's helped out some people in town when needed, but he only works with people he likes who are innocent. No more criminals.

Jack asked me why Phoenix thought I needed someone to check on me and I couldn't stop the smile on my face. Knowing that he cared enough to make sure that I was okay makes me feel valued and protected.

I told Jack about my ex knocking on the door and how Phoenix saw it all. Told him everything ugly thing my ex said. It was good to have someone other than Phoenix to talk to.

Sharing my story seemed to send Jack into protective mode. He advised me that my ex can't legally demand the money for the wedding, and if he tries anything, I should let the police know.

A week ago, I would have said it was unlike Chad, that he'd never do anything like that. But after his performance on my doorstep, I'm not sure I ever really knew him.

As I turn into Phoenix's driveway, I try to push all of this out of my head. I want to concentrate on him. This feels like a date.

He wants to take me to one of his favorite places, even if it means hiking instead of the traditional dinner and a movie.

I get the feeling that Phoenix doesn't do anything the traditional way. Especially after that kiss last night. It wasn't a traditional first kiss, but holy hell, what a kiss. I'd never known a kiss could feel like that. It kept me up most of the night, replaying it over and over in my head. It's a wonder I got *any* sleep because thoughts of that one kiss had me so turned on.

Phoenix is sitting on the front porch as I pull up at his cabin, and he stands to greet me as I get out of the car.

I give him a shy smile as I hold up my camera. "Is it okay if I bring this? You never know what we might come across, and I hate to be without it."

His smile dims, but he nods. I know I'm using it as an excuse to have something to fiddle with and focus my attention on other than him. When things get too intense, I find myself needing a distraction.

Reaching into my car, I pull out my hydration backpack that Jack insisted I bring on any kind of a hike out here.

"I packed a lunch and some snacks," Phoenix says as he pulls his hydration backpack over his shoulders and secures it. Then he slings a rifle over his back. It doesn't faze me because I've learned that with all the wildlife out here, it's more common for someone to carry a gun than not.

"Thank you for dinner, by the way. Jack stayed and ate with me, and it was nice to not be alone, so thank you." I want to make sure he knows I appreciate what he did for me.

He steps up to me and takes my hand in his. "You don't have to thank me. I'll always make sure you're okay and taken care of." As he says this, he stares me right in the eye.

Those words would have meant a lot to me no matter how he said them, but having his eyes on me makes them even more poignant. "Thank you." It doesn't seem like enough but it's the only thing I can think of to say.

He keeps hold of my hand as we walk down a path behind his cabin.

"So, where are we going?" I ask.

Not answering me, he just turns and smiles. I guess I'll see when we get there.

The walk itself, even though we aren't talking, is extremely calming. Listening to the sounds of nature is soothing. The birds, the small animals, the rustling of leaves. and the crunch of our footsteps. The further we hike into the woods, the more relaxed I get.

I have no camping or outdoor experience besides hiking in a couple of national parks, so I should be nervous, but I trust Phoenix. This is his land, and I have faith that he knows every inch of it.

"What's the most interesting animal you've ever run into while out here?" I ask.

"A few years ago, I ran across a mother bear and two baby cubs by the river. The mother sat on the riverbank and the cubs played in the water. Until they leisurely walked off, I stayed and watched the whole thing. The only other experience that ties with that one is the pack of wild horses that runs through here. There are several valleys on my land that they like to graze in, and I'll usually see them once or twice a year."

"That's amazing."

We hike for about thirty minutes until the trees open up to a breathtaking view of the mountains and the river below. We're up a slight cliff with the river below us and a path down to our right. In front of us, a hammock is stretched between two trees, looking down the river to the mountains beyond.

"May I?" I hold up my camera and he hesitates for a moment, then nods.

I snap a few photos from behind the hammock and the view beyond it so you can imagine yourself sitting there and what the view would be.

After taking a few photos, I put my camera away, and Phoenix relaxes again. I've picked up that, for whatever reason, the camera makes him nervous, but I'm grateful for the pictures he lets me take.

He takes the packed lunch out of his backpack and sits down in the hammock facing the river. "Come join me." He pats the spot next to him.

Setting my backpack down next to the tree, I join him on the hammock.

"I can't say I've ever sat in a hammock before, but I'm officially a fan. The view is absolutely beautiful, and the company is pretty good, too."

That causes a smile to fill his face as he hands me a sandwich.

"So, how often do you come up here?" I ask him as we eat our lunch.

"At least once a week, if not more. I get my best ideas for the things I create for the shop here."

"I bet watching the sunset or sunrise is breathtaking, especially when you see the lights bounce off the water in the mountains." I can almost see in my head how perfect and relaxing it would be.

We spend some time talking about the spot–how he found it, and the different things he's seen sitting up here.

Long after we finish our lunch, we continue to sit in comfortable silence, letting the breeze wash over us. It's as if the wind up here sweeps away all your problems and leaves you feeling refreshed and renewed.

Sitting here with him, I'm aware that my entire left side is pressed up against him from shoulder to knee. Since I'm pretty sure he's flirting with me just a little, I decide to take a chance, especially after our kiss last night. I simply rest my head on his shoulder and continue staring out at the view. He tenses for just a moment, and then relaxes, taking my hand in his.

"There's supposed to be a storm rolling in tomorrow morning. It'll be raining for most of the day. Then the following day I'm planning on going hunting. You should join me. Bring your camera because you never know what you'll find exploring after a good rainstorm," he says as we swing slowly in the hammock.

"I'd like that. What time do you plan on leaving?"

"7:00 a.m."

"I'll meet you at your place. We should probably start heading back. I have dinner plans with Emelie and Axel tonight," I tell him.

"In town?" he asks as we stand up and start collecting our stuff.

"Yes, at the cafe on Main Street. Dinner is going to be just Emelie and me, but Axel is bringing her into town. She said not to freak out if he stalks us." I laugh and shake my head.

When Emelie said it, I guess my surprise showed on my face because she was quick to reassure me that it's just Axel's thing. He'll watch over us, but stay far enough away so we can have our time together. As I thought about it later, I found it kind of sweet that he wanted to make sure she was okay.

"He's very protective of her, and when you're with them, he'll be just as protective of you," Phoenix says.

"It'll take some getting used to. I'm used to controlling, not protective." I realize I've said too much, and immediately turn and grab my stuff.

"Too bad I didn't bring my suit. The river would be a great place to take a dip," I say, changing the subject.

"You don't need a suit." He gives me a wicked grin, making his way down to the water.

CHAPTER 8

JENNA

I follow him, wanting to see what he's going to do. When he gets to the riverbank, he looks back at me before pulling off his shirt and dropping it on the ground.

"Are you trying to get me to go skinny dipping?" I smirk, and his cheeks turn a cute shade of pink.

He shrugs, undoes his pants, and lets them fall to the ground. Stepping out of them, he jumps into the river in his boxer briefs. Damn, I wish he would have let me get a better look at him. I also wish I'd had time to snap a picture.

When he pops up for air, he turns to look at me with a question in his eyes.

Will I join him? No question about it. A chance to get closer to an almost naked, sexy as hell mountain man? Yes, please.

I decide to give him a show. I slowly remove my shirt and let it fall next to his. Phoenix stops moving in the water, his eyes glued to me as he waits to see what I'll do next.

Not disappointing him, I remove my shoes and socks and set them next to his. Finally, I unbutton my pants, sliding them down my legs until I'm in just my bra and matching panties. His eyes go wide but he says nothing. His gaze roams over me, and not in a creepy way, but more like he's appreciating everything he sees.

I have a sudden thought. This bra isn't one I should get wet in the river. It was my last big splurge on my parent's credit card, and I can't replace it if it gets ruined.

I turn around and undo my bra, setting it on top of my shirt. There's a soft gasp behind me. I cover my breasts with my hands, turn back toward him, and walk into the river.

Only once the water covers my chest do I drop my hands.

"That bra cost a fortune and I can't afford to ruin it in the river water," I say, trying to explain my choice away.

It suddenly dawns on me that the water is much warmer than I anticipated. It feels like the water you would expect walking into a heated pool, minus the chemicals. "Why is the water so warm?"

"H-hot Springs," he chokes out.

His eyes are still locked on me as I take a few tentative steps toward him. I stop when I'm within arm's reach, but he doesn't move. The heat in his eyes and his heavy breathing are the only signs that he wants this as much as I do.

I take two more small steps toward him, but he still doesn't reach for me. Did I read him all wrong? Does he not want me?

"Do you want me to leave you alone?" I whisper, not sure I want the answer.

Phoenix shakes his head "no" as his eyes trail to my chest hidden under the water line. I can see the want and need in them. Maybe he just doesn't want to scare me off.

"You can touch me."

His eyes shoot up to mine. I want to wrap my arms around his neck and press my chest to his. And I very much want another kiss, but I know in my gut he needs to make the next move, whatever that move is. So, I stand there and wait as he rakes his eyes over what little skin he can see above the water.

At first he's hesitant to touch me, but when he finally does, it's possessive. Pulling me to him, his arms wrap around my waist, and I collide with his body. His hard, muscled chest bunches and flexes against me, making us both moan.

Staring into his eyes, I wrap my legs around his waist and wind my arms around his neck. His hands go to my ass as he kneads the skin.

Not waiting for him to kiss me, I make the next move. My lips have barely touched his before he takes control of the kiss. His hand runs up my back and presses me even tighter to him, and then I feel his hard length between us. My pussy is throbbing and wet, and not just from the river. I need a release more than I need my next breath, so I wiggle my hips against him to see what his reaction will be.

When Phoenix groans and pulls me tighter against him, my core throbs in anticipation. Then he grips my hips and slowly starts moving my body over his length. It feels so good that all I can do is moan. Finally breaking our hot as hell kiss, he pulls back to watch me as he sets a steady, delicious pace.

The friction is exactly what I need. Every time he hits my clit, it sends tremors through my body. My hard nipples rub against his chest hairs, playing with them, sending shivers over my body. The sensations overwhelm me, and I don't realize he's moved us to the shore until my chest is out of the water.

Phoenix's eyes are on my breasts, making my nipples tighten in anticipation. Breaking his rhythm, he lifts me in one powerful move and takes my hard nipples into his mouth.

"Oh! Fuck, that feels so good," I gasp, breaking the silence between us.

He gains confidence with each of my moans, sucking harder as I try to move my hips again. But he holds me in place, easily overpowering me in the best way.

He moves his lips back to mine and starts grinding my hips over his cock again, which I swear is even bigger than before. This time the pace is fast and more frenzied.

When he breaks the kiss and rests his forehead on mine, I'm worried he's going to stop. So I pull him closer, holding onto him tightly.

"I'm so close. Don't stop," I gasp.

Thankfully, he doesn't. His hands grip my ass harder, picking up the pace. He's holding me so tight I know I'm going to feel it for days. The pain mixes with pleasure and it's enough to send me over the edge screaming his name. When his mouth closes around my nipple again, it kicks my orgasm up to a level I didn't know existed. Clawing at his shoulders, I need something to hang onto, to ground me as the most powerful orgasm I've ever had overtakes me.

I hear his grunt and feel his orgasm as his whole body shudders. I finally float down from my high, my body boneless in the aftermath. I rest my head on his shoulder, and he moves us further into the water to keep us warm.

He lightly rubs his hands over my back, letting me relax against him. Then, noticing the nail marks on his shoulder, I lean down to softly kiss them. Each time my lips touch him, he shivers, and goosebumps race across his skin.

"I needed that so bad. Thank you," I say with a smile, kissing his neck.

"I'm pretty sure I should be thanking you," he chuckles.

We stand there for a few minutes as he runs his hands over every part of me he can reach. After a few minutes, he gives me another short kiss before we make our way back up to the shore to get dressed.

His eyes are glued to my chest, and I can't take my eyes off the outline of his big cock in his boxer briefs. The water has them painted to his skin, hiding nothing as it grows, tenting his underwear. Knowing he's getting hard for me makes me want to drop to my knees and worship him with my mouth, but I don't want to overwhelm him. He wants to take things slowly, and I'm willing to go at whatever pace he sets.

Slowly, we both get dressed, each watching the other. We need to head back to the cabin, or we'll have a repeat of what just happened.

"Lead the way." I try to break the tension.

Phoenix nods, and we gather our stuff from the hammock.

The return journey seems quicker than our trek out to the river.

I turn to find Phoenix watching me once I've put my stuff into the car. Giving him a playful wink, I take a step towards him.

"I had a really good time today. Thank you for showing me your spot where you go to relax. It was just what I needed today."

"Anytime you need to relax, just let me know. I'm happy to take you out there again." He moves closer, taking my hands in his and pulling me against him.

I like this more confident side he's showing me. A flirty Phoenix is as hot as hell and I know I'll be taking care of myself in my bath tonight because he already has me soaking wet again.

Now there's barely an inch between us, and I can feel his body heat coming off of him. I want nothing more than for him to kiss me, and thankfully, he doesn't make me wait long.

He leans in, kissing me just as softly and gently as he did yesterday. Wanting to get closer, I wrap my arms around his neck, and he pulls me against him. There's no hiding how hard he is and it's good to know I have that effect on him.

"How am I already addicted to kissing you?" he whispers against my lips.

I don't have an answer for him because I feel the same way, so I just keep kissing him. Time seems to stand still and speed up at the same time. I don't want to stop kissing him, but the more turned on I get, the more I know I should put a stop to this.

When he finally breaks the kiss, we're both out of breath. He doesn't pull away, resting his forehead on mine. "Have a good dinner with Emelie. Stay home tomorrow. Don't try to go out in the storm. I'll see you the day after to go hunting." He finally takes a step away from me and opens my car door.

"I can't wait."

Getting in my car, all I can think about on the way home is how I'm excited that we have plans again so soon.

It doesn't hit me until I pull into the driveway that I've never been hunting before and I have no idea what to expect.

CHAPTER 9

EMELIE

"Calm down, Little One, she won't be here for a few more hours," my husband says.

My husband.

I still believe I get to call this amazing man my husband for the rest of my life.

"Yes, I know. But it's been so long since I've met a girl I could be friends with. I was never good at making friends in school," I say as I check the table setting.

I decided to have Jenna come over instead of meeting at the Café. Thankfully, Phoenix was able to get my message to her.

"Her decision to be your friend doesn't rest on whether the table is perfectly set or not," Axel says.

I know he's right, but fussing over the table gives me something to focus my nervous energy on, and Axel is trying to distract me.

After looking over the table again, I go into the kitchen to check on dinner and make sure that I have everything I need.

"Come sit down with me, Little One. You've gone over everything at least four times now. Let me help you refocus your energy."

"None of that before she gets here." I smile at him. As much as I would like to sit on his lap and get lost in my husband, Jenna will be here soon, and I need to go change clothes.

Thankfully, Axel follows and changes into the clothes I laid out for him. If it's just us around the house, we wear old clothes. His jeans have holes in them, and I hardly ever wear a bra nowadays, but those clothes aren't suitable for company.

I do love it when Axel dresses up for us to head into town. He looks sexy as hell in dark jeans and a button-down shirt with his sleeves rolled up showing off his tattoos.

The knock on the door comes just as we finish getting dressed.

"See? I told you no time for fooling around," I smirk at him.

"Wait here."

Axel never lets me open the door, even when we know who it is. Like today, when we're expecting someone. I think it's partly his need to protect me, and partly because of the time my ex showed up, followed by the cops. He worries for me.

A moment later, Jenna steps into the living room, and her eyes go wide as she looks around our house. "Wow! This place is amazing,"

"Axel built it all by hand. He's started expanding out the back, and it's a sight to watch." I wink at my husband, who blushes slightly.

He's such a big guy, and he still can't believe how attractive I find him. It's one of the reasons the expansion of the cabin is slow going because at least once a day I'm dragging him to the bedroom. Simply watching him gets me so damn turned on.

"Come sit down. We have a little time before dinner is ready. How are you liking Whiskey River?" I ask as we take a seat in the living room.

"You sit and chat. I'll finish dinner." Axel kisses the top of my head before going into the kitchen.

I had a feeling he would do this when he insisted I make a meal he knew how to cook, too.

"It's so beautiful and calming here. It feels like home," Jenna says.

I smile. "I know what you mean."

I go on to tell her how I ended up here after my ex left me in the woods when we were camping. I found Axel, and we were stranded in the cabin for a week before I even got to see the town.

"By the time I made it into town for the first time, I instantly felt at home, and knew this was where I was meant to be." My loving gaze finds Axel in the kitchen who returns my look.

Jenna watches him hesitantly.

I place my hand on her arm. "He's a big teddy bear, sweet and loving, but he's protective of those important to him," I reassure her.

"Phoenix seems the same way. You know he had Jack check on me one night and bring me dinner?" she asks with a warm smile.

My eyes meet Axel's for just a moment. We both know there's more to the story. Something happened if Phoenix went as far as to ask Jack to check on her, but we won't push to get anything out of her that she isn't willing to tell us.

"Phoenix is protective of us all. He always makes sure we have what we need and that we're okay after big storms."

"Dinner's ready," Axel says, carrying plates of food to the table.

As Jenna walks over to the table, she pauses, looking it over closely. "Phoenix made this table, didn't he?"

Surprised, I turn to look at Axel to verify because the table was already here when I met him.

"He did," Axel says.

"How could you tell?" I ask in shock.

"He's been letting me hang out in his workshop as he works, and I noticed he does the corners like this." She runs her hand over the table.

"He made our bed frame and dresser, as well," Axel says, nodding his head in approval, although I'm not sure why.

As we begin to eat, we talk about Jenna's photography and the book she has planned. Our conversation flows into questions about what the winters are like up on the mountain.

"I'm glad to have another girl around. I hope you'll stay," I tell her as we finish dinner.

A flash of something crosses her face, but it's gone so fast I'm not sure I even saw it.

"I don't want to be rude, but you should go while there's still some daylight to get you down the mountain," Axel advises.

"Thank you. I'm still not familiar with the area, so I don't like driving at night," Jenna says.

"Let's do lunch in town one day when the guys meet at the shop." I want to chat with Jenna again, and get to know her better.

She nods and smiles. "I'd like that."

We say our goodbyes, and Axel walks Jenna down to the gate while I clean up from dinner. I'm washing dishes when Axel comes back in, and a moment later, he wraps his arms around my waist from behind. His front presses to my back, and his warmth surrounds me. He always makes me feel safe.

"This dress was a tease all night at dinner, Little One," he growls into my neck.

I lean back into him as his hand travels up my leg and under my dress.

"So was this shirt, My Giant." I turn in his arms and run my hand over his chest before slowly unbuttoning it.

His hand continues to move upward, knowing he won't find any panties in his way. He's made it clear he likes easy access to me and anytime I wear panties, he rips them from me and refuses to let me replace them.

I only get two buttons undone before he makes contact with my clit. I gasp and lose my train of thought. He picks me up and sets me on the edge of the kitchen counter before unbuttoning his pants.

I love watching him when he's like this, in need of me. As much as I love our fun around the house, I need something more tonight.

"Take me to the river, My Giant."

CHAPTER 10

PHOENIX

The storm yesterday was about as bad as I expected. So, I decide to start the day by radioing the guys to make sure they're okay. With all the rain, there's a good chance the road to Axel and Emelie's will be washed out for a few days. I know they're more than prepared, but I still want to check.

I start with Bennett, since he's the furthest one out. I get the radio going and call him.

It takes a few minutes to get a response. "Hey, Phoenix. I know you're checking in after the storm. I'm perfectly okay. Not even any downed tree branches."

"Good to hear. Stay safe."

Short and to the point. That's how we roll.

Next, I call Cash. I'm saving Axel and Emelie for last because Emelie will want to know how the other guys are doing.

As with Axel, it takes Cash a few minutes to get to the radio. "Hi, Phoenix."

I know it's a radio and not the best connection, but he sounds worn out. Things can't be easy with his brother being sick. "How did you fare in the storm?"

"We're good here. The storm made my brother more paranoid than usual, but I gave him some sleeping medicine and he slept the day away."

"What do you need? What can I do?"

It's a solid minute before he replies, and I know he's thinking carefully. "He's not himself anymore, and I can't leave him alone. If you have time to pick up the stuff and take it down to the shop, it would be greatly appreciated. We don't need anything else."

"I can get up there sometime next week. Before I show up, I'll set a more concrete time."

"Thank you."

Now, on to Axel and Emelie.

"Hey, Phoenix. I was waiting for your call. Axel's out checking the road now," Emelie answers.

"Other than the road, you guys okay?"

"Oh, yes, we're good. We won't ever complain about having to stay inside and snuggle by the fireplace."

It's easy to see the love those two have for each other, and they don't hide it from anyone. I'm so happy that Axel found Emelie, and I hope one day I'll find someone for me.

Jenna's face flashes in front of my eyes, and there's a flutter in my heart that hopes she might be that one. But she doesn't know my story and I don't know all of hers. Plus, there's a good chance she's only hanging out with me for her book and for a little fun. I have no problem with that, but I have to guard my heart as it's been broken too many times.

"If the roads flood, do you guys need anything?"

"Well, I'd kill for some Oreos right now, but I'm not going to make you drive into town for them. I'll wait until we can go ourselves."

Emelie grew up in Billings and was used to being able to head to the store for all the modern conveniences. She's transitioned well to mountain life, but she still has her favorites that she misses. If we're honest, I think we all do.

"I'll call Jack and have him place a bulk order for you. Then you won't have to worry about running out anytime soon."

"Why didn't I think of that? Genius idea. Thank you, Phoenix. How did you fare in the storm?"

"Found some downed branches around the house which would be perfect for the decorations I was thinking about making. I checked on the other guys. The storm aggravated Cash's brother, but otherwise, everyone fared pretty well."

"Axel just walked in, and he said the road is passable in an emergency but should be cleared up in a day or two. It didn't flood as bad as we thought it would."

"Well, you two stay safe, and let me know if you need anything."

Jenna should be here anytime now, so I start checking my gear. It's been a while since I went hunting because I was working on the latest order. Yesterday's storm lasted until the afternoon, and I'm anxious to check out my land.

As I get ready, I have a nagging worry that Jenna won't show up, or she'll change her mind. Then I hear her car in the driveway, and my nerves ease, leaving excitement at seeing her in their place.

As she steps out of the car, she says, "So, I realized when I got home, I probably should have told you I've never been hunting before... "

I figured as much seeing as she's basically a city girl. But as much as I'd like to get in a kill today, I just want to spend some time with her.

"Have you ever shot a gun?"

"Yes, a handgun."

"Good. Wait here." I head into the house to get my handgun.

At least she can use it to protect herself out there if needed. I plan to take care of her, but you can never be too careful, especially if I end up bringing an animal back.

Stepping back outside, I find her messing with her camera, but she stops when she sees me.

"Carry this with you just to be safe."

She frowns. "How will you bring back whatever you kill?"

"There are a few meadows close by that deer like to feed in after a good storm. If we don't find anything closer, I'll try further out another day."

We load up our gear and the packed lunch I prepared for us before heading off down a different trail to the one we took the other day.

"How was your dinner with Emelie?" I ask as we walk.

"Oh, it was so nice to have a girlfriend to chat with. She told me how she and Axel met. It's horrible that her ex just left her in the woods, but fortunately, she stumbled upon Axel. The way he looks at her, you can see they were meant to be. It's so sweet. Having a friend like Emelie gives me hope that something like that is out there for me."

This would be the perfect opportunity to tell her she's found it with me, that I will always protect her. Running from her ex brought her to me, and I'm pretty sure being that upfront would send her running again. Slow and steady, that's how my dad won my mom over. What I wouldn't give to have his advice right now.

"Emelie is a good person. She takes care of all of us and is always sending us home with food. I've put on ten pounds since they got married. Yeah, I wish I was joking but I'm not. Her food is so damn good, I won't let it go to waste."

"She told me she's excited to have another girl around, and it made me feel guilty because I didn't tell her about my ex. We were having a good time, and I didn't want to bum her out or worry her."

"You should have told Emelie. Axel will help protect you. So will Cash and Bennett."

"Why? I'm no one special. I'm just starting to be friends with Emelie."

I stop on the trail and face her. "They'll protect you because you're important to me." I stare into her eyes, trying to make my point. With everything in me, I need her to understand what I'm not ready to say and what she probably isn't ready to hear.

A beautiful shade of pink coats her cheeks, and her breathing increases slightly before she nods her head.

As I keep walking, I make notes of some of the trees that look like they're ready to come down. I can come back and stock up for winter so I'll still be able to work in my workshop.

Pointing them out to her as we go, I explain some of the different pieces I could make. Even though she's snapping pictures, she doesn't slow me down, nor does she ask me to stop and wait. She keeps up, knowing I don't want her to get separated from me.

We make it to the meadow where I'm pretty sure I'll be able to find some deer, and we sit down on the edge and wait.

After the fog clears from the meadow, we don't have to wait long before the deer appear on the other side, just along the tree line. I hold my finger to my lips, silently telling Jenna to be quiet, and she nods.

Moving into position, I line up a shot and wait. As they come a little bit further from the tree line, my shot becomes clearer. Not much time passes before I fire. A deer goes down and the others scatter.

"You did it! Wow, I've never seen anything like that. I'm so glad I remembered to turn all sound off on my camera." Jenna holds the camera screen to me, showing me photos of the deer she took while I was lining up my shot.

"Those are great," I tell her, not at all shocked at how good her photography is.

Carefully, we walk to where the deer went down and check to make sure the blood hasn't drawn any predators.

"Always scan the tree line because the blood will draw in everything from wolves to coyotes to bears," I tell her as we finally make it to the deer.

Making quick work of gutting the deer, I get it ready to carry like a backpack, which involves removing some bone from the legs. I expect her to flinch or be grossed out or even turn away, but she watches every move and takes photos as I work.

"What's that for?" she asks as I tie an orange band around the deer.

"This is my land and there shouldn't be anybody on it. But that doesn't mean people pay any attention. So the orange is basically a signal to other hunters that I'm a human carrying a deer, and will prevent them from trying to shoot this deer."

Once I have the deer ready, I tie up the hide and make backpack straps out of it. I slide it onto my back and stand up.

Jenna watches me in awe before she speaks. "I had no idea how that was done."

I gather up my gun and we head back to the cabin. I'm on extra alert because the blood will attract predators, but Jenna is too, with her camera forgotten and her hand on the gun she's placed in the waist of her pants.

We make it back to the cabin without incident. Out back, I have a workshop that has a table where I process all the meat and animals. It's further away from the cabin, so if the blood draws anything, I'd be safe.

When we enter, Jenna takes a look at everything. I have hides hanging around. There's a table in the middle for me to process the animal, all sorts of tools, shelves for storage, and a sink.

"I hope you're not squeamish," I say with a smirk.

CHAPTER 11

JENNA

"I hope you're not squeamish," Phoenix says as he sets the deer on the table, a playful grin on his face.

There are lots of windows in here and tons of natural light, but he also turns on the overhead light.

"No, I did some volunteer work in the emergency room. At one point, I wanted to be a doctor. I saw some pretty horrible things there."

"What changed your mind about being a doctor?" he asks as he starts pulling out different tools.

"It's a lot of money to go to medical school, and the more money I borrowed from my parents, the more control they had over me. I was at a friend's house one day, and her dad did photography as a hobby. He started teaching me, and I fell in love with it."

I don't tell Phoenix how upset my dad was when I told him I didn't want to be a doctor anymore. After that, my dad decided my only use was in marrying me off. But Phoenix doesn't need to worry about how horrible my parents were. *Are.*

I spend the next several hours watching in fascination as he skins and butchers the deer. He's very patient with me as I ask questions, and explains why he does certain things. He always saves the hide and uses it to make blankets or on his furniture. Every possible part of the deer is put to good use.

Phoenix shows me how he wraps the meat ready to store in his freezer for the winter. I love watching him through the lens of my camera. He's confident with his knife skills, and it's obvious he's in his element. I'm not going to lie, it's sexy as hell.

He keeps looking over at me every so often, like he's expecting me to faint from the sight of blood. But it doesn't bother me, even if I did cringe when he pulled out the deer's guts earlier. I have no clue what I'm doing, but he lets me help where I can.

"Where did you learn all this?" I ask, thinking maybe he was taught by a family member like his dad.

"Well, I watched a lot of videos online. If I need to learn how to do something new, I find a YouTube video or something. Bennett has taught me so much, like how to carry the deer and the best ways to process it. I learned quite a lot about hunting from him, particularly hunting in this area. He's an amazingly skilled tracker."

I want to ask about his family because I'm curious, but then I'd have to be open to him asking about mine, and that's the absolute last thing I want to talk about right now.

As Phoenix works in silence and while his attention is on the deer, I focus my attention on him. His arms are big, muscular, and strong, but he's gentle as he handles the deer. The way he was able to get the hide off all in one piece was impressive.

He's very patient, especially with me as I ask so many questions. He's a little bit awkward from spending so much time out here away from people, but it's a quality I like about him. It's refreshing that he's honest and real, not a fake version of himself.

He's different from the guys I grew up with, and fortunately, very different from my ex. Where Chad wore a suit to work every day, Phoenix has no problem wearing worn, ripped jeans, and a T-shirt. With his muscular build, he looks so much better in it than Chad ever did in a suit.

Chad paid a hundred dollars for the perfect haircut and spent more than me on hair products to make sure not a hair was out of place. He would shave every morning and was meticulous about his appearance.

Phoenix is a direct contrast to Chad. His hair is a little longer as if he's gone a while between haircuts. It has a slight curl at the edges. Phoenix will go days without shaving and he looks hot as hell, but I've seen him shave his face too, and no matter which way he goes, he pulls it off.

Spending sixty to eighty hours a week in an office meant Chad's skin was paler than mine. Phoenix's skin is tan from his hours spent outside, and the rough calluses on his hands felt amazing on my body the other day.

Taking a deep breath, I change my train of thought. Just thinking of our skinny dipping adventure has me turned on, and I'm craving Phoenix's hands on me again.

"I just have to put it in the freezer. Would you like to stay for dinner? I was thinking of grilling a couple of these venison steaks. There's nothing like fresh venison on the day it's caught." Phoenix has a huge smile on his face, and he looks like a kid in a candy store.

"I'd love to stay if you're sure it's not a problem."

"Come on, help me get this meat into the freezer and I'll get dinner going."

As we step into his cabin, it's not at all what I was expecting. I knew he had electricity based on what I'd seen in his workshop and the solar panels on the roof. But the interior of the cabin looks like it could be in town and not miss a single amenity.

We walk in the side door, which takes us directly into the kitchen. The kitchen is U-shaped and looks out over the living room and dining area. The logs Phoenix used to build the cabin form the walls, and he's mixed in stone as a splashback and along the kitchen island.

"Go ahead and have a look around. I'll go get the last of the meat," he says on his way outside.

Stepping into the living room, I see the fireplace, which is a showstopper with its rustic stone surround. On the far wall overlooking the rear of the cabin are floor-to-ceiling windows that showcase the amazing view of the mountains.

The large U-shaped couch looks like the most comfortable place in the world, filled with pillows and blankets. Depending on where you sit, you'll have a great view of the fireplace or a fabulous view out the window.

Following the hallway down the side of the house, the first room I come across is a library that also looks out over the rear of the cabin with more mountain views. The walls to my left and right are nothing but shelves filled with books. In the center is another couch that looks just as comfortable with pillows and blankets.

On the coffee table sits the book I assume Phoenix is currently reading. Typical guy, into action and James Bond stories. I walk around to one of the walls of shelves and start looking over the titles. Everything from classic Jane Austen to the complete James Bond collection, poetry, and anything that you could imagine on local animals and plant life.

"I see you found one of my favorite rooms in the cabin."

I look up to find Phoenix leaning against the door frame watching me. "How many of these books have you read?"

"On that wall? All of them. And on the other wall, just the ones on the top two shelves."

My jaw drops because that's easily several hundred books.

"Let me show you my favorite place in the entire cabin." He holds his hand out toward me.

I take it, following him further down the hall into what I'm sure is his bedroom. When we step into a bathroom, I gasp because this is instantly my favorite place in the house, too.

More floor to ceiling windows look out over the same breathtaking mountain view as the living room and the library. Right in front of the windows is the most beautiful, oversized clawfoot tub I've ever seen. It's positioned so you can gaze out over the vista while you soak. Like the rest of the house, the bathroom is decorated in wood and stone and it's the most relaxing place I can ever remember being in.

"When I was building the cabin, I knew I'd want someplace to soak when my muscles were sore after a hard day of work. I considered a hot tub, but that's a lot of upkeep, and I thought maybe..." He trails off and a blush covers his cheeks.

It's the sexiest thing I've ever seen. "Maybe what?"

"I thought maybe someday my future wife would prefer a clawfoot tub to a hot tub." He shrugs his shoulders like it's not a huge deal.

"Well, as a woman who loves a nice bath, I can tell you that you one hundred percent made the right choice."

That causes him to smile, and he seems to relax.

I follow him out as he starts dinner, taking the opportunity to look around the living room some more.

Several photos sit on the fireplace mantle. There's one of Phoenix taken at the shop in the town with Axel, Cash, Bennett, and Jack.

There's another of him standing in front of a partially built cabin. But the one that catches my eye is the one in the middle. It's of him and, I assume, his parents. He can't be more than a teenager in this photo, and he looks nothing like the mountain man he is today.

They're dressed up for some event. He's in smart pants and a button-down shirt. His father is wearing a sports coat, and his mother is in a fancy dress with her makeup and hair done up. It's easy to see Phoenix's resemblance to his mom and dad.

"Those are my parents," he says as he steps into the living room and sees the photo that I'm holding.

"Do you still talk to them?"

"No, they passed away in a car accident. They were caught in a storm on the way to my eighteenth birthday."

I gasp. "Phoenix, that's horrible! I'm so sorry. Is that when you moved out here?"

He nods, hesitating for a moment like he's trying to decide how much to tell me. "Not only was I an awkward kid, but I was also an only child. I didn't have any friends. When they died, I inherited my dad's company, the one I was set to take over, but had no interest in running. It sold for more money than a kid at eighteen should ever have at his disposal. I used the money to buy two hundred and fifty acres out here and built the cabin. I've been here ever since. This life suits me. Even if my parents hadn't died, I would've ended up out here."

I don't hear much more of what Phoenix says. All I can think about are the smaller details in the photo–the designer dress, the expensive watch and lavish jewelry.

Phoenix is from the world I've been trying so hard to escape. He's from a world where money is used to control people, where no one cares about your feelings, just what you can do for them.

Even though I know in my heart Phoenix is different, I have to separate myself from that life and any connection to it if I'm going to have a chance at being on my own–– truly, completely on my own.

As painful as it might be, that means I have to separate myself from Phoenix.

CHAPTER 12

EMELIE

I've been cooking for two days now, making a bunch of casseroles and meals to fill Cash's freezer. Everything from meatloaf, chicken casserole, spaghetti casserole, to simple mac and cheese. I even included his favorite huckleberry pie and some fudge brownies.

Axel hasn't said a word about all my cooking, though he's enjoyed sampling it. But there's something I need to talk to him about, and I don't think he's going to like it.

"Hey, sexy," I call out to him from the kitchen.

He's sitting on the couch in the living room watching me and pretending to read, even though he hasn't turned the page in over half an hour.

"What do you want?" He sets his book down and looks at me suspiciously.

"How do you know I want something?" I make my way over to him and sit on his lap.

"Because you only call me sexy when you want something you know I'm not going to like." He wraps his arms around me and pulls me even closer to him.

Just as I do every time I'm on his lap, I melt into him. He rubs my back and kisses the top of my head, waiting for me to ask him. He hasn't told me no on any of my crazy ideas yet, but that's not to say he won't start now.

"I want to go with Phoenix when he takes the food to Cash. I want to check on him, and see what else we can do to help."

I wait for him to think it over. One of the things I love about Axel is he considers everything carefully, especially when it

comes to me. He knows that this is important to me.

"We'll go together. Let's go get ready-
. Phoenix will be here soon."

Instead of jumping up, I turn, straddle his
waist, and kiss him with everything I have.
I want him to know how much this means
to me, how much *he* means to me.

"Little One, we don't have time for this. If
you want to go, we need to get ready," he
groans, but doesn't push me away.

"Tonight," I say as I stand up.

"Tonight," he agrees, and follows me to the
bedroom.

We have just enough time to get ready before Phoenix is knocking on the door. As
always, Axel answers it, his body tense and
one hand on his gun. He relaxes as soon as
he confirms it's Phoenix.

While I get the food ready to take down
to the truck, they have a hushed conversation. I know Axel is telling Phoenix my idea,

and when I hear him chuckle, I know he's agreed.

"I made you and Cash a huckleberry pie," I say, holding up his pie.

His eyes go wide. "You know I won't pass that up. What can I take?"

He jumps right in, helping to carry the food to the trucks at the end of the driveway. Hopefully, all the food I prepared should last at least a month.

Phoenix takes his truck, and we follow behind in ours. I've never been to Cash's home, and I've never met his brother, so I'm a little nervous. But I trust Axel, and I know he won't let anything happen to me. If he thinks this is safe for me to go, then I'll place my trust in him.

We pull up to a cabin about the size of ours before Axel started the addition. I jump out and help Phoenix with the casseroles just as Cash steps outside. He stops short because I know he was only expecting Phoenix.

"I just wanted to visit and see if there's any way I can help. Feel free to tell us to leave.

We don't want to be a burden," I say, waiting for him to let me know what he's comfortable with.

"I could use the company." He turns to go back inside.

I look at Axel, who nods. He grabs the last of the food, leaving Phoenix's pie in his truck, and we follow Cash inside.

The cabin is clean, but there's medical stuff for his brother everywhere.

"My brother is asleep. He's not in any condition for visitors," Cash says, coming to a halt in the living room. He looks nervous.

"Cash, we're here for *you*. What do you need? Taking care of him can't be easy. What can we do to help? Cleaning? Dishes? Laundry?" I ask.

He glances around but looks hesitant to ask for what he needs.

"What can the guys do? Do you need firewood? Need meat for winter?"

"Bennett brought me a few animals. But I do need wood. I can't get outside long enough to chop any."

"I'm on it," Phoenix says, and heads back out the door.

"We'll be on cleaning duty," I say, not giving him a choice.

"I'll do dishes," Axel says.

I start gathering clothing to do a load of laundry. I silently pray these guys don't live so far off the grid they don't have a washer and dryer.

When Cash starts picking up stuff in the living room, I place my hand on his. "I know it's hard to accept help. But please let us. Go lay down, get a nap, take a shower, do something for yourself so you can recharge. It's the best way you can help."

He stares at me for a moment before he nods and heads for the bedroom.

I do some cleaning and organizing, not moving anything too far from where it is so Cash knows where to find it. Axel joins me as I fold laundry, and he finishes up the cleaning. When Phoenix starts bringing in some of the chopped wood, Axel helps him.

Quietly as possible, we finish up just as Cash's brother starts making noise.

Cash checks on him and quiets him down before stepping back out to talk to us. He looks around at what we've done, and I can tell from the sheen in his eyes that he's fighting his emotions. "Thank you. I... Thank you," he says, his voice choked.

"It's what we're here for," I reply with a shrug. "There are meals for the next month in the freezer. All the directions for cooking are written right on the top. There's also a pie on the counter. Call if you need any-thing at all, otherwise, we'll be by the same time next month with more food." I step up slowly and hug him tight.

He pats my back. Even though I know he's not used to a lot of affection, everyone needs a hug now and then.

"You two go on. I'm going to get the stuff for the store before I head out," Phoenix says.

Axel and I leave, and we barely get out of Cash's driveway before Axel is pulling the truck to the side of the road.

"What's wrong?" I ask, checking the area around us to see what I missed.

Soon as the truck is in park, he unbuckles my seatbelt and pulls me into his lap.

"You knew what he needed, and you did it in a way he was able to accept. Thank you. You show me over and over again just how much you were made for this life."

He places a kiss on my lips, and I pull back because what I want won't happen on the side of the road. "Take me home. We need to finish what we stated earlier." Smiling, I slide back into my seat.

"Be prepared to be spoiled. You won't be leaving the bed for a few days," he growls as his hand lands on my leg.

I still can't believe this is my life. It's better than anything I could have hoped for.

CHAPTER 13

PHOENIX

I'm loading up my stuff to take into the shop today. I got the stuff from Cash and checked in on him yesterday. After Axel and Emelie left, I was able to check on his brother, too.

His brother is a lot worse than I expected. He won't be around much longer, which is sad because had he gone to the doctor, he could have been treated and lived a long full life. Cash has never been on his own. After their parents died, his brother took him in and moved them to their property in the mountains.

His brother is crazy smart and holds some pretty famous patents, but he's paranoid. Because of that, Cash has been fairly isolated other than coming to the shop. I'm worried how he'll do once his brother is gone, so I made sure he knew he had us, and now Emelie, too. We'll make sure he's okay.

Even with Cash and his brother on my mind, Jenna isn't far from my thoughts. She's been pulling back since she had dinner at the cabin and I'm hoping to get Emelie's take on it from a female perspective. Yesterday didn't seem the right time to ask her. I'm not sure what to do. I don't think I did anything wrong. We barely kissed that day, and she was fine after our swim in the river. My mind has been going over every detail for a few days now as she slips further and further away.

Heading to the shop to see the guys is a welcome break. I walk in and unload mine and Cash's stuff. The guys and Jack notice.

"Cash isn't able to leave his brother's side. He's paranoid and isn't himself. Cash is keeping him comfortable with some sleeping medicine, so he had me bring his stuff in."

"That explains the meds he had me order. They came in yesterday," Jack says.

"I can take them up to him. You good to settle his account?" I ask, knowing Jack should be able to make any bank deposits he needs for him.

"Yes. Just let me get it all set and I'll print out a receipt for you to take to him," Jack says, turning his attention to his computer as Emelie and Axel walk in.

"How's he really doing? Since you stayed a bit longer, I'm hoping he opened up to you," Emelie asks.

"He looks tired and worn out. To be honest, he could use some of your sweet fudge. I'll be taking this up to him in a few days so I can stop by and pick some up."

Emelie's eyes light up. "We'll go to the store and get what we need," she says with a smile on her face, which of course, makes Axel smile.

"What's new with you two?" I ask them.

"Not much. I'm still learning everything I can and preparing for winter. How's Jenna?" Emelie asks.

"I don't know. We went hunting a few days ago, then I invited her for dinner, and she's been pulling away ever since."

"Maybe it was your cooking," Bennett says with a chuckle as he walks over to us.

Emelie gives him her death stare before turning back to me. "Okay, walk me through what happened."

"Well, she did great on the hunt and even after, when I was skinning and butchering the deer. She took photos, asked questions, and the only time she cringed was when I was gutting the deer. I asked her to stay for dinner and she wandered around the house while I put the venison steaks on the grill and put the meat away."

"What did she find when she was wandering the house?" Emelie asks.

"She looked through my books in the library and the photos on my mantle. She saw one of me and my parents and asked about them, and I told her the truth." I cringe because other than knowing that they died when I was young, I haven't told the guys all the details. "I told her they died on their way to my eighteenth birthday party."

Emelie places her hand on my arm. "I'm sorry, Phoenix."

"That's why you hate birthdays," Bennett says, putting two and two together.

I nod. "I told her when they died, I sold the company and bought the property out here and I've been here ever since. That's when she started pulling away."

The guys know my parent's company sold for a lot of money. Bennett and Jack both helped me set up my portfolio because as a kid of barely nineteen when I got here, I had no idea I shouldn't keep over a billion dollars in the bank.

"Most girls run toward money, not away from it," Axel says.

"From what she told me that night you had me take her dinner, I put a bit of her past together," Jack says thoughtfully. "She's accustomed to people in her life using money to control her, and that's why she moved out here."

Now it all makes sense. Her ex showing up and demanding money. The mentions of her trust fund, and not using her parents' money.

"If that's true, she's probably running away because she thinks you're from the life she left. You have to show her you aren't like the people she's trying to get away from," Emelie says.

"Go explain how your parents were. Tell her to look them up. There's enough online about the type of people they were," Bennett says.

"Most importantly, if you're sure she's it for you, don't let her run and put space between you. She'll be used to people not putting in the effort, so if you have to camp in her front yard, do it. Don't let her push you away," Emelie says.

The conversation carries on around me, but I don't hear any of it. I'm making plans to visit Jenna. Maybe I'll go get lunch and take it to her since it's still early. After I've loaded up the stuff for Cash in my back seat, that's what I'm going to do. But first, I'll need to stop at the Café.

What if she sees the fact that I paid off her ex as me being just like her parents?

· · · · ● · ● ● · · ·

Jenna

After selling one of my large prints online, I went into the city yesterday and bought a couch and a TV. I was getting pretty bored in my cabin. They just delivered the couch this morning, and it's so soft and plush I'm sure it's more comfortable than the mattress on the floor I've been sleeping on.

I also bought some throw pillows and a blanket to go with the couch, along with a stack of books I got at the thrift store here in town. So now I'll not only have a place to watch TV, but I have a reading area, too.

This place is slowly starting to feel more and more like home. I'm saving up now to get a security system installed. If Chad knows where I live, my parents will, too. I don't want to be caught off-guard again.

Just as I'm just settling in to read a book, there's a knock on the door, making me wish I'd bought the security system instead of the couch.

My heart races as I walk to the door, a bit scared of who I'll find on the other side. Hesitantly, I open the door to find Phoenix standing there looking nervous.

"Phoenix?"

"Can we talk? I brought lunch." He holds up a paper bag.

When I step aside to let him in, he hands me the food and stops short when he sees the couch. It's not easy to miss since it's a large L shape. The light gray color that works well with the wood cabin walls really sold me on it.

"I finally got a couch. Try it out. It's the most comfortable couch I've ever sat on," I tell him.

He takes a seat at the end closest to the door. I sit on the opposite side so I can face him.

"The couch is perfect for you," he says before looking back up at me. "What scared you off?" He gets right to the point.

There's no reason to play dumb and make him explain when I know exactly what he's talking about. I owe him the truth. "Where I come from, money means power, and people use that power to make you their pawns. It's why I couldn't be a part of it."

"I know that life, and people like that, but it was never my family. Even though we had more money than others, we were the outcasts. Look up my parents, Thomas and Quinn March. They owned March Enterprises out of Billings. They specialized in technology for my dad and real estate for my mom."

He stands up and walks to the door, then stops. "I'm going to go check my fishing lines tomorrow. If you want to come with me, I'd love to have you. If not, I understand, and I won't bother you again."

Before I can reply, he's out the door, and I'm left alone.

He wasn't here that long. I'd think I imagined him if it weren't for his scent lingering in the air. As I eat the sandwich he brought me for lunch, I pull out my phone and search his parents on the internet.

The first headlines are all about their death.

'Billionaire, Thomas Quinn killed by Drunk Driver: Son, Phoenix set to inherit company.'

'Can the 18-year-old heir of March Enterprises really run the company?'

'March Enterprises sold in one of the largest deals the state has ever seen.'

Scrolling back several pages, I look for articles about his parents before they died. None of the articles mention Phoenix, and that eases my mind a little. They didn't force him to be in the media to better their image like my parents did.

'March Enterprises to restore historic Montana Homes.'

I read a few articles talking of the work his mom was doing to preserve the past and the historic homes even though they didn't make her any money. My mom doesn't do a damn thing if it doesn't benefit her.

'March Enterprises turned down governor's invitation to dinner.'

Reading the article, I find that Phoenix's parents refused to dine with the governor after it was revealed he was having several affairs and got two women pregnant at the same time. Neither of them was his wife. His wife chose to stay beside him, as many political wives do. The Marches are quoted as saying how appalled they were about his behavior and would not support it. The governor was not reelected, and the politicians tried to blame it on them.

'Thomas and Quinn March spend a week working hands-on remodeling an orphanage.'

This is the first time I find a photo of Phoenix. He was sixteen and helping his parents. The orphanage suffered damage in a tornado, and while all the kids were fine, they didn't have the money to do the repairs. Not only did his parents fund all the repairs, they spent a week getting dirty on-site, cleaning up, and helping with the rebuild. Another article goes on to show the final project and how they made sure all the kids had their own beds and a new toy waiting for them when they reopened.

The people I know would've thrown money at the orphanage and never thought of them again. No one I grew up with would have gotten their hands dirty like that.

I spent many more hours reading headline after headline about a family who truly cared and had morals. How different it must've been to grow up that way, to be allowed to be a kid and have fun instead of posing for press photos every weekend.

Phoenix's family was different, and the worst part is how he lost them so young. The world needs more people like his parents and fewer people like mine. For an instant, I wonder how different his life would-'ve been were it my parents that died instead of his. I scold myself. No matter how much I hate my family, it's never good karma to wish death on anyone.

Thinking of my parents, I do a quick search on them. The headlines lead me to find that Chad is already engaged again, this time to Tami, who was to be my maid of honor. We have forced friends—forced by our parents, but not really close. I think I'd be more surprised if Chad didn't go after her. He's in it for the money and to social climb. After mine, Tami's is the next best family to marry into. It makes sense.

It also makes sense that he wanted the money he lost on our wedding if he had to help pay for another. As I stare at their engagement photo, all I can think about is that he'll be on affair number three or four by the time they have their first kid. If she's lucky, they'll have two separate houses and only be together for events. The life of the rich behind the cameras.

I can only imagine the money his parents spent on the press campaign after I called off the wedding, and how fast Chad moved on. Because all the post-wedding articles say he left me because he realized he was in love with my maid of honor, that I'm hiding because I'm embarrassed about being left at the altar. My parents are quoted as saying they wish them all the happiness and blessings they deserve. In my world, that's a huge fuck you and may karma do its worst.

The press campaign easily cost his parents millions because there isn't one mention of me leaving him. With how fast he moved on, for all I know, he could have been cheating.

Yep, the world Phoenix grew up in is miles away from the one I know.

I suddenly realize it's dark, and way past dinnertime. Going into the kitchen, I put dinner in the microwave and think about Phoenix. If I hadn't seen those articles, if he hadn't told me about his parents, I would never have guessed he came from money. He doesn't act like it, which has to mean something. My gut says he's a good guy and nothing like the people in the world I grew up in.

Tomorrow he wants me to join him fishing, and he made it a point to say he won't bother me again if I don't go. So essentially, if I don't show tomorrow, I would be saying it's all too much and I'm done. It's an easy out. But is that what I want?

When the timer goes off with my food, I grab it and sit at the kitchen island to eat. Then I pull up my phone and search for information about fishing lines so I don't look like a complete idiot out there tomorrow.

CHAPTER 14

PHOENIX

Today I'm loading up for a trip out to the river. I'll be checking my fishing lines and putting them back out again, because I have about a week where I can gather the best fish to store for the year. Even though I can fish with a fishing pole any time, I prefer to fish with the lines. But I only have a small window. So, I've been out fishing every day this week, and I was hoping Jenna would join me today, but it doesn't look like she'll be here.

I packed a lunch for us, and plan on taking the four-wheelers along with a trailer hook-up. It means traveling, but I can bring more that way. I wait half an hour past when she should be here. I was hoping she'd see my family was different, and that I was different. My parents didn't want me hanging out with people who acted like Jenna's social circle for precisely the reasons she ran.

If Jenna can't see I'm not controlling, that I'm different from her parents, I hope over time I can show her. I check my watch again. I can't wait any longer, so I double-check my gear one more time and get ready to head out. Just as I sit on the four-wheeler, her car pulls into the driveway.

I stand, but I don't move toward her car. I need to make sure she's here to spend the day with me, not to let me down in person.

Jenna gets out of her car and we both stare at each other for a few minutes. Neither of us moves or speaks, but so much is said between us in other ways. Jenna is studying me as if seeing me through new eyes. I'm not sure if that's a good thing or not.

I see a woman fighting to stand on her own two feet, even though it's not the easiest path. She could've had all the money she ever needed or wanted. A society wife do-ing whatever she liked. But that isn't her. She wants the path less traveled, and she wants to do it her way.

Breaking the spell, she reaches into her car and comes out holding up her camera. "I thought I could take some pictures with you today?"

For just a moment in the back of my head, there's a warning bell telling me the only reason she wants to spend time with me is for the photos and to get more info for her book. But I push that thought away to worry about later. Right now, I want to simply enjoy her being here.

"That's fine. Ready to go?"

She nods, and I secure her helmet. Being this close to her again makes me think of our time at the river, and I wonder if I can get her in the water again today. I probably shouldn't push my luck.

Climbing on the four-wheeler, I help Jenna to sit behind me. Good lord, I don't think I thought this through. She's sitting with her chest pressed up to my back and her arms wrapped around me. My mind goes everywhere but on where we should be going.

I decide to take the longer route to the river to see if we can get her some good photos. We reach a hill that looks down over a field where I know a pack of wild horses likes to hang out this time of year. I park the four-wheeler and help Jenna off. After only taking a few steps, we can see the wild horses grazing in the field.

"Phoenix, they're beautiful," Jenna says in awe.

She watches them for a few minutes before beginning to take photos. Most of the horses in this pack are a different shade of brown, but there are a few black and white ones, and some painted ones as well.

"Is this your land?" she asks as she pauses to take photos.

"Yes, from the road at the base of the mountain to the river on this side. The other side is trickier, but there are markers if you know what to look for."

"It's beautiful. I can see why you settled here."

"The moment I stepped on the property, I felt at peace. At home. I spent the first year exploring it and fell in love with it even more."

We watch the horses for a while before I speak again. "The man who owns a hundred acres on the other side of the river is putting his property up for sale. I'm thinking of buying it."

"Are there good trees there?"

"I'm sure there are, but it could be a lot to get them across the river. He has great hunting, though. There's a small cabin on the property, too, but I'm not sure what I'd use it for."

"Too bad you don't like people. Tourists would pay a pretty penny to stay in a cabin out here."

I grunt at just the thought of it. "I don't want strangers on my land day in and day out. It's a good way for someone to get shot while hunting. Come on, we need to get moving."

We load back up and make our way to the river. As I stand at the river, I think about what it would be like to own the land on the other side. Right then, I decide to make him a generous offer. It's not about making money off the land. It's about the life I want and if I want to expand my family, be it with Jenna or someone else down the road, then I need to expand my land, too.

· · · · ● · ● · · ·

Jenna

Does Phoenix have any clue what riding on the back of these four-wheelers while pressed up against him is doing to me? I should have worn a thicker bra because my nipples rubbing against his back is turning me on more and more with each bump. My clit is throbbing for release, and the vibrations from the motor aren't helping one bit.

When we finally reach the river, I can't wait to get off and put some space between us.

Hopefully, I can calm down. The fresh air seems to help, and he's more than willing to take a few minutes to relax before breaking the silence.

"Let's have lunch before we work on my nets," he says, pulling food from his backpack.

This time it's a BLT sandwich, and what looks like homemade potato chips.

"You make these chips yourself?"

"Yeah. I have a garden, and the potatoes produced well this year. Had to find a way to use them." He shrugs like it's no big deal.

I'm finding Phoenix to be a man of many talents, and everyone I meet I like just as much as the last.

We lean against the four-wheeler and watch the river as we eat.

"You know," Phoenix says, "when I was younger, I had no idea we had money. My parents never acted like we did. Yes, we lived in a nice house and had a pool. If I needed clothes, they provided them for me. But I wasn't given everything. If I wanted a video game, I had to work for it. It wasn't until I went to one of the kid's birthday parties from my class and I saw their house that I realized I lived differently. That was about third grade."

I stay quiet wanting to listen to whatever he wants to tell me.

"Sixth grade was when kids started to notice my family came from money. I'm not sure if it was what they heard from their parents or if they realized my stuff was named brands, or what. That year, I had a bunch of friends and I slowly started to see that they were there because they wanted stuff from me. When I wasn't blowing money on them, giving them expensive gifts, or taking them to do things, they stopped being my friend."

"Kids are shitty at that age. I think it's a requirement for middle school to suck for everyone."

Phoenix gives me a smirk before losing himself in his thoughts again."By high school, I was an outcast. The rich kid who wouldn't spend money on people, whose parents wouldn't deal with their parents' games, and who was okay being alone. Besides my neighbor, an eighty-two-year-old World War Two veteran, I didn't have any friends. But I loved hearing his stories. We had lunch together every weekend and dinner once or twice a week. I'd help him around his house, and my parents would pay me an allowance for it. No more than ten dollars a week, though."

Finishing my sandwich, I wrap my arm through his and rest my head on his shoulder, offering him comfort in hopes he'll keep going with his story.

"Just as I started my senior year of high school, he passed away. I graduated a week before I turned eighteen. My parents were throwing me a party and while it was mostly their friends attending, I was excited. They had a meeting run late, and were on their way to my party when a drunk driver hit them. They died before EMT was even on the scene. I had no one. The day after the funeral, I woke up and just drove until I ended up here. I met Jack that day, who took me under his wing and introduced me to Bennett. They helped me out. I sold everything and moved here. They helped me go to school online and taught me how to manage my money."

"I'm so sorry. That's a lot for anyone to go through, much less at a young age and all on their own." More than anything, I want to tell him he won't ever be alone again. But I'm not ready to make those kinds of promises. "My childhood was the exact opposite. As young as I can remember, I knew we had money and my parents loved to spend it. I went to preschools, and it was a sport to see who was richer, who could get their parents to buy them the newest this or that. I learned how to manipulate my parents because to them, status was everything. It was around middle school when I started to see how fake everyone around me was. My best friend was my best friend because her parents and my parents told us we were. It was then I realized I didn't have any true friends."

Phoenix doesn't say anything, just turns and kisses the top of my head where it's resting on his shoulder.

"By high school, I learned to work the system. As long as I stayed out of trouble and was the perfect society daughter when they needed me, I was able to be a kid. Go to football games, parties, prom. I had a teacher that took me under her wing and taught me all the advanced things I know about photography as an extracurricular class. She helped me convince my parents that taking advanced photography classes and using what I knew to volunteer would be a great way to stand out on college applications, so they agreed. It did help, and I received several scholarships. Even though I got a full ride to NYU, my parents demanded I go to Colorado State University, so I was close to home and could come back on weekends."

I was so mad at them, and that's when I promised myself I'd find a way out. No matter what.

"So, I went and took as many photography classes as I could. I even majored in it without my parents finding out. Of course, they lost it when they realized I graduated with a degree in photography. That's when they set me up with Chad. Insisted it was time for me to settle down. I liked Chad at first. He was charming and sweet. We had fun together, and I think at one point I thought I was in love with him. So, when he asked me to marry him, I agreed. The moment I agreed, he became a different person. I got so lost in planning our wedding, I didn't see it. Then we were standing there at our rehearsal, and he didn't once look at me. He was barking orders at everyone but could care less about me. That's when it hit me. I watched him that night. He became this new person I didn't know, and it was clear he was marrying me for my family's money."

My train of thought falters when Phoenix shifts, pulling me so my back is to his front and wrapping his arms around me. He leans on the four-wheeler and I rest my head on his shoulder, soaking up his comfort as I continue where I left off.

"That night, when everyone was planning my wedding, I slipped one of the waitresses a few hundred dollars to keep telling people I was across the room, or had taken a phone call from the florist, or was in the bathroom talking to a bridesmaid. Anything wedding-related to buy me as much time as I could to get home and pack up my car. It took me less than an hour before I was all set to leave. I was across the state line before they blew up my phone. Even though I turned it off, I guess they found the letter I left. That first day in the store they called me, but then I changed my number and heard nothing until Chad showed up at my door the day you were there."

"Have you heard from anyone since?"

"No. I searched my parents last night when I was looking up yours. Chad's family did a great job spinning the whole thing. It must have cost them millions to get every paper to report that Chad left me at the altar because he realized he was in love with my maid of honor. They're engaged to be married now. She was the best friend my parents told me was my best friend. The papers all said I was so heartbroken and I left to 'find myself.' Nothing about him cheating or what really happened."

"I'm glad you're here now. And I hope Whiskey River starts to feel like home for you. You seem to be settling into your place," Phoenix says.

"I love my little house, but being out here with you gives me a sense of freedom I've never experienced before. I keep trying to find the perfect picture to capture it or a way to describe it, but nothing comes close. "

"Sounds like the mountain has taken another soul. You'll never be the same again," he says with a chuckle.

I know I won't ever be the same, but it's not because of the mountain. It's because of this mountain man.

CHAPTER 15

PHOENIX

When we start to check the fishing nets, things seem different between us. Jenna hasn't picked up her camera and is helping me, asking questions about fishing and how I plan to store the fish. There's a decent amount from this run, so I'm glad for the help and, of course, the company.

On the way back to the cabin, feeling her pressed up against me has me harder than steel. I haven't had someone in my space like this in years, and while I thought it would be uncomfortable, I find I crave it. Every time I use the four-wheeler, I'll think of this moment.

We spend the next hour getting the fish into the smoker. I'd be able to do it faster on my own, but Jenna likes to learn, and I like teaching her how I do things. When we step back outside, the sun is starting to set, and the weather has cooled off.

She takes a deep breath and smiles at me. My heart almost stops at how beautiful she looks. Even after a hard day preparing for winter, she's still smiling.

"I'm jealous of your life out here." She looks over at my cabin.

"Why?" I find myself wanting to know all her thoughts, and I'm asking her just as many questions as she's asking me today.

"It's so simple. Back to basics. It's a big reason I chose to do this book in Montana. Everything is slower paced than it was in Denver."

"It's why I like being out here, too." Looking at her, I can see she's much more relaxed than the first time I saw her in the store.

"Would you like to stay for dinner?"

"Yeah, I would."

Reaching out, I take her hand and lead her back to the cabin.

"I pulled out some chicken this morning. What would you think of grilled chicken?"

At the mention of chicken, she gets this little twinkle in her eye, and she walks over to the pantry and steps inside. Not sure what she's doing, I turn to follow her, but she's already walking back out with a few things in her hands.

"How about I make you my nan's chicken casserole?"

"You want to cook for me?" I ask, slightly shocked.

"If that's okay. If not, I promise no hard feelings."

"I haven't had anyone cook for me since my parents passed. Emelie sends me home with pies or cookies when I'm over there, but it's not quite the same."

"Is that a yes?"

All I can do is nod. I don't think she realizes how big of a deal this is for me and how much it means to have this little bit of her wanting to take care of me. "What can I do to help?"

"You can park your cute butt on that stool and keep me company while you direct me to where things are." She points to the barstool at the kitchen island.

My face heats at her calling my butt cute. She knows exactly what she's doing because she gives me a wink and turns back to the stove.

We talk while Jenna gets the casserole ready. Staying on happy topics, she tells me about her nan, who sounds like the happiest part of her childhood until she died her freshman year of high school. I tell her about the early years here on the property and how much I had to learn.

Once the casserole is in the oven, Jenna works on making some rolls, and mashed potatoes for a side.

She pauses and looks at me, giving me a shy smile. "Now we wait. Dinner should be ready in about twenty minutes."

"Come here." I hold my hand out to her and she comes willingly.

I pull her into me so she's standing between my thighs, our upper bodies sealed together as she rests her head on my shoulder. It's comfortable, and I love having her in my arms, wherever we are.

That's the moment thunder shakes the house. Her head pops up and a vise squeezes heart at the thought of her driving in this after dinner.

"It might be best for you to stay here tonight instead of trying to drive back to town."

Jenna watches me for a moment, then nods. "I think you're right. I don't know the mountain well in good weather, so I certainly don't want to try to navigate it in a storm."

Her agreeing to stay here calms me. Then my nerves jangle for a whole new reason. She'll be sleeping under my roof tonight, in the room next to mine. I won't get any sleep, but will gladly give it up if it means she's safe.

As we sit down to dinner, she watches me intently as I take the first bite. The casserole is a creamy mixture, and the chicken almost melts in my mouth. It's easily one of the best things I've eaten, besides steak, in a long time.

"I think this is my new favorite food," I tell her and she beams a huge smile.

Over dinner, it becomes obvious how easy things are with Jenna. I've always had to work at relationships. Even with the guys, it's hard. But with her it doesn't feel like work, it feels natural as if she was meant to be here.

"Would you like to take a bath and watch the storm? Maybe read a book?" I ask her after dinner.

She fights a yawn. "I think I want to go to bed. It's been a long day and I don't remember the last time I was this tired. I'd probably fall asleep in the tub."

"Take a shower in my bathroom, and use whatever you want. I'll get you something to wear and leave it on my bed."

She nods and closes the bathroom door.

Taking a deep breath, I pull out one of my t-shirts for her. This will have to work for tonight as my pants would fall off of her. I leave it on the bed, close the door, and go to the library to wait for her.

If she's going to be spending more time with me, it might be best to have her leave some clothes here. But those thoughts are killed the moment I realize she's naked in my shower.

I imagine she's using my soap, rubbing it all over body and those gorgeous tits. I've only been able to see and play with them once but they've starred in my dreams every night since. All I can think about is soap and water running down her naked body.

Minutes later, Jenna appears in the door-way wearing my shirt, hair tousled from her shower, cheeks flushed, and looking sexy as hell.

"I'm sorry I don't have anything else to fit you," I say as I run my eyes over her. The shirt is huge and falls to her knees but is thin enough I can see her nipples are hard.

"Let me show you to the guest room." I stand, not even hiding when I adjust myself. A move she doesn't miss.

She walks right into the room and sits on the bed. I want her in my bed, but I don't want to scare her, and I don't want to make things weird. Knowing she hadn't planned to stay here, it's best to give her space.

"Good night," I turn to leave.

"Phoenix?"

Her voice stops me, and when I turn around, she's standing again.

"Can I have a goodnight kiss?"

"Do you even have to ask?" I don't mean to say it out loud. How could she think otherwise?

I cross the space between us in two large steps and pull her into my arms. For just a moment she stares up at me before standing on her tiptoes to kiss me. My intention is for a sweet, soft goodnight kiss, but when she wraps her arms around my neck and I feel her hard nipples rubbing against my chest, it's like my body has a mind of its own.

I run my hands down her back to grip her ass, and she moans into the kiss. Lifting the shirt, I touch the bare skin of her ass, and it's as if cold water hits me. I've never thought of taking the next step quite like this, and I want to be with her more than anything. But I'm a virgin, and saying I'm nervous is an understatement. I gently pull back from the kiss, and when she looks at me, her eyes are dazed.

After helping her to bed, I place a kiss on her forehead before heading to my room and right to the bathroom. Making sure the door is locked, I strip and get into the shower. Without a second thought, I take my cock in my hand and start stroking. Even though I'm constantly hard around her, knowing there was nothing more than my thin shirt separating me from her was too much.

Just imagining what would've happened if I'd pulled that shirt from Jenna and laid her down naked on the bed, has me even harder. I think about sliding into her the first time. I want my first time to be her, and every time after. Thinking of her moaning my name while I'm inside her sends me over the edge and cum shoots from my cock, hitting the shower wall and going down the drain.

After showering and getting ready for bed, I check the house to make sure everything is secure, especially with Jenna here tonight. Once in bed, I notice the house seems different. I can hear every noise, and I listen to the storm, wanting to make sure everything is okay. That Jenna is okay.

I'm not sure how long I lay there before my door creaks open.

"You awake?" Jenna whispers.

"Yeah. Everything all right?"

"Yeah, I just can't sleep. New house, new sounds, and knowing you're in here."

Scooting over, I hold up the blanket. She scurries over and climbs in, cuddling up to me. I wrap my arms around her and hold her close.

"You're nice and warm." She snuggles into me until there's not an inch separating us, and I hold her even tighter.

She places a kiss on my chest, then looks up at me. I lean down to give her another kiss. I should know by now that kisses with this girl quickly get us carried away. No sooner are my lips on her, than her hand begins wandering over my chest. I run my thumb over her hard nipple and when she moans, I feel it in my cock.

Her hand heads south, and I grab it, pulling away from the kiss.

"Nothing more than kissing tonight. It's been a long day. Get some sleep. I'm right here and I'll keep you safe."

She sighs, but nestles into me and rests her head on my chest. It isn't long before her breathing evens out and I know she's asleep. Not only do I want her more than my next breath, I want her here in my house, in my bed, every night.

The problem is, I'm still not sure if she's here for me, or for her book. Until I know for sure, I can't give my virginity, or my heart, away.

CHAPTER 16

JENNA

Before I even open my eyes, I know I'm not in my own room. The bed is way too comfortable, and I seem to have my own personal heater. Opening my eyes, the first thing I see is Phoenix, who I'm wrapped around. This brings a smile to my face. What a way to start the day. What girl wouldn't want to wake up wrapped around her own personal mountain man?

After enjoying the sight of him for a moment, I slowly attempt to maneuver out of bed. When I try to move his arm off me, he just tightens his hold. I change gears, moving my legs off and slowly sliding from under his arm, which works. After finger combing my hair, I decide it's the best it's going to get, but still looks like a wild mess.

I head into the kitchen, poking around a bit, and deciding to make him breakfast. Omelets and bacon and some quick biscuits. I also get the coffee going.

I'm standing in front of the stove, waiting to flip the last omelet when strong arms wrap around my waist from behind. Phoenix kisses my bare shoulder where the shirt has slipped down and presses his hard, muscled body to my back, including his very hard cock.

"I didn't like waking up to an empty bed," Phoenix murmurs against my neck.

"You had a death grip on me, so I had to use my best ninja skills to get out so I could make you breakfast. If you hadn't woken up, I was going to bring you breakfast in bed."

"Waking up to you cooking breakfast for me is second best."

After he sits down, I begin plating everything and set it at the kitchen island for us to eat. He pulls my chair as close to him as he can get it and wraps one arm around me, holding me to his side. It's as if he can't keep his hands off me. I like it a lot, so I snuggle into him.

"There was something I wanted to ask you-," I say, suddenly nervous about putting words to the thoughts that have been swirling around my head all morning.

It's been like pulling teeth to get him to open up, and I know it's the same for me. We both have so much in our pasts we'd rather keep buried. But at some point, we also know we have to talk about things. If I ask Phoenix questions, I have to be open to answering his questions.

"What's that?"

My nerves are on high alert, and there are millions of butterflies in my stomach. My fight or flight is shouting to run away or, at least, abort and change the subject. Pull off something silly and keep the mood light.

Instead, I take a deep breath and jump off the cliff. "Why did you stop when we were kissing last night in bed?"

His grip on my hip tightens, and he takes a moment to finish the food in his mouth before answering me. Every second that ticks by feels like an hour, and I almost get up and start cleaning the kitchen for something to do.

"You know my story. I didn't date in school, and I haven't dated since I've been out here either."

I think he's going to add more to explain what he's trying to say, but he doesn't. Maybe I don't have enough coffee in me because it takes longer than it should to put the pieces together. If he hasn't dated, does that mean he hasn't done other things? Guys have one-night stands all the time. I'm sure there isn't a lack of tourist women in the summer who would love a vacation fling with a sexy mountain man like him. Surely he isn't...

"Are you...?" Not sure how to ask, I pause.

"I'm a virgin. Hell, you were my first kiss since we appear to be having this discussion." He starts to remove his arm like he's going to crawl back into his shell.

But I'm not going to let him.

I grab his arm and snuggle into him even more. I wait for him to relax before I go on. "I'm honored to have been your first kiss, and if it helps, I would never have guessed it was your first. You're a really good kisser."

His face turns from pink to bright red, not just red, but bright tomato red.

I rest my head on his shoulder. "I like that you're a virgin, too. A part of you no one else has gotten. If you choose to go that far with me, I'd be honored. But I won't push you. Just know if and when you're ready, I'm ready. Actually, I'm ready all the time around you."

His breathing quickens. "You are?"

I move his hand from around me and slowly up my thigh. His eyes are glued to where his hand is disappearing under the shirt. When his fingers come into contact with my bare pussy, he inhales sharply but doesn't say a word.

I spread my thighs in invitation. "Feel how wet I am? I'm always like this around you."

His eyes shoot to mine. Slowly, he moves his fingers against my clit, and it feels so damn good. He doesn't miss a single thing. Based on my reactions, he adjusts his movements, and in no time at all, he's driving me crazy. When he slides a finger into me, my restraint slips. I close my eyes, losing myself in the sensations he's causing.

When I open my eyes again, he's still watching me, but there's a small smile on his face. Yeah, he's pretty freakin' good at this, and now he knows it. I try to hold back my orgasm to allow him time to play, but it's like he knows what I'm doing, and he doubles his efforts.

I give in and grab the counter in front of me as I come. He doesn't stop moving, drawing my orgasm out until I'm over-sensitive. Only then does he pull his fingers from me and bring them to his mouth, licking them clean.

"Wow," he says, leaning forward to kiss me softly. "That was…"

"Amazing," I finish breathlessly.

He presses his forehead to mine. "I should check the road for you."

He doesn't move, and neither do I. Neither one of us likes the idea of me leaving right now.

He got to play, and now I want to take my turn. But when I reach for his hard cock, he grips my wrist and stops me. Bringing my hand up to his mouth, he places a kiss on the center of my palm. His lips are soft, and my hand tingles from his touch. The gesture is so sweet and caring. I don't think anyone has ever given me this kind of attention.

He looks up and his eyes lock with mine. The air around us seems to sizzle for a moment before he clears his throat. "I was thinking of going hunting again today."

Though I want to go, this time I want to go for *me*. Not for the book, or photos. I want to go and learn. Maybe fool myself that this could be my life someday. Lord knows I want it bad enough.

"I'd like to go with you. This time I want to learn to hunt. No camera."

When I mention leaving the camera at home, a brilliant smile takes over his face. "Let's do it." He scoops me up into his arms.

Gasping, I wrap my arms around his neck as he carries me to his room, and we get ready to head out. I put on my clothes from yesterday and he loans me some camouflage. It's like we've been doing this for years. Getting ready to go out together is so easy and fun. For a moment, I wonder if this is a brief glimpse of a life I might have, and I know right then I want it more than anything.

After getting everything together, we go outside, and Phoenix gives me a quick lesson on using the hunting rifle in case I need it for protection. Then we're off to a different meadow to the one he showed me the last time. It isn't long before I realize this trip is more about spending time with me, and me not leaving today, than it is about our hunting.

"If you wanted to spend more time with me, you could have just said so. I didn't want to leave either," I tell him.

The shy smile I love covers his face. If he only knew the things that smile does to my body, he'd use it daily as a weapon against me. I'm so turned on I'd let him throw me down in the mud and have his way with me if he just gave me that smile.

"Will you stay for dinner again tonight? Tomorrow, I'll go check the roads for you."

I nod in reply, taking his hand as we leisurely walk back to the cabin. "So, tell me. What are winters like up here? From what I've heard, tourists stop passing through around Labor Day, so there are probably fewer people."

"Yeah. Though, we get winter tourists starting in December or after our first big snow. They're the people who like winter sports, but it's nowhere near like it is now. The guys and I normally get snowed in for most of the winter, so we prep and plan for that. We plan so we don't have to make it to town until spring. None of us like fighting the mountain because it ices over and can be treacherous."

"Do you have a snowmobile to get around with?"

"Of course. Otherwise, there's no way I could stay in the cabin for months on end. In the workshop, I have a stockpile of wood so I can keep working. Come spring, I always have a large load of stuff ready to take down to the shop."

"Do you think Jack would be willing to see if some of my prints sell? I can frame them. Maybe include some local shots?"

"I think that's a great idea. Tourists love local stuff. Things to take home to remind them of their time here. It's why Jack's shop does so well."

"I'll run it by him and see what he thinks."

We talk more on our way to the cabin, and he seems to relax more and more with each step we take.

As for me, each step feels more and more like home, and that's a dangerous feeling.

CHAPTER 17

JENNA

We make dinner together. I love the little routines we're developing. His cabin feels like a home. I like mine, but I'm still trying to piece it together. This place is well lived in, and it's completely him. I wonder if my place will ever have that feeling.

No matter where I go in this cabin, I'm comfortable. At my place, I don't have that just yet. Maybe someday I will, but I think part of me has always known it's temporary.

Phoenix observes me throughout dinner. I catch him watching the little things, like how much food I take, and how I arrange my plate. I wonder if he's filing notes away for later. How he'll use them, I have no idea, but I'm excited to see what he'll do with that information.

After dinner, we wash the dishes. I'll never like washing dishes, but I like standing in the kitchen with Phoenix.

"Want to watch some TV?" he asks once all the dishes are done.

"I'd love to, but if you don't mind, I want to take a shower first."

"Of course. Let me get you another shirt to wear."

I follow him into the bedroom and take the shirt from him. We both stand there and look at each other, not sure what to say.

"Feel free to join me anytime." I wink at him, which makes him blush.

I turn and go into the bathroom leaving the door unlocked. I know he won't join me, at least, not tonight. But I hope one day soon he will because I'd love nothing more than to see all those muscles he hides under those worn clothes.

As I shower, I try not to think about what it would be like to have him in here with me, but my mind can't seem to go twenty seconds before flashing back to Phoenix naked and dripping in water.

I consider trying to give myself an orgasm, but with Phoenix just down the hall, I decide against it. In the end, I leave the shower pretty damn turned on. Tonight, I decide to see how far he's willing to go. I need some relief, and if he's feeling anything close to what I am, he's going to need some, too.

I find Phoenix in the living room on the couch.

"I put in a comedy movie. I hope that's okay," he says, trying not to make it obvious that he's looking at me.

It's no surprise he's looking at me. This shirt is thin, and I'm not wearing anything under it. Plus, I'm just out of the shower.

"That's fine. With any luck, we won't be watching much TV." I smile and make my way over to where he's sitting on the couch.

I stop in front of him, letting him get a good look at me. I don't want to push him too far, but at the same time, I want to encourage him. When his eyes meet mine and the same heat I feel is mirrored in them, I have my answer.

I straddle him and his hands go to my hips as he watches me, waiting to see what I'll do next. I can feel his hard cock between my thighs, so I brace my hands on his shoulder and move my hips. His eyes roll back and his head falls onto the couch. When he looks up at me, I do it again.

"That feels so good," Phoenix moans, gripping my hips tighter.

"Yeah, it does." I lean in and kiss him.

When I roll my hips again, he groans, but he's still tense.

"Do you want me to stop?" I don't want to push him too far.

"No, God, no."

"You tell me when to stop." I grind against him.

His breathing quickens and his dick gets even harder. "I'm not going to tell you to stop." He holds my hips in a death grip.

"Don't tease me. If you mean it, I'm going to demand you remove all your clothes right now." I'm half-joking, but it's more of a tease.

He calls my bluff and whips off his shirt, pushing me to stand in front of him before I realize what is going on. Then he starts to pull off his pants but looks at me hesitantly.

I grip the hem of the shirt I'm wearing and slowly pull it up. With every inch of skin I reveal, he watches me closely. Finally, I pull it over my head and let it drop on the floor with his.

Phoenix is frozen in place, staring at my naked body. I would be self-conscious with anyone else, but with him, I can see the hunger and desire in his eyes because he doesn't hide it. It's so refreshing.

I lean forward and start pushing his pants down slowly, giving him time to stop me, but he doesn't. His hard cock springs free, and all I can think about is licking the pre cum dripping from it.

I push him back down to the couch and fall to my knees in front of him. When I push his legs wide, he watches my every move but doesn't stop me. Wrapping my hand around the base of his cock, I stroke him a few times before leaning forward and running my tongue over his tip.

"Oh, fuck," he gasps, gripping the edge of the couch so hard his knuckles turn white.

Pulling back enough to look him in the eye, I ask before going any further, "Do you trust me?"

"With my life," he says seriously.

This time I don't go slow, swallowing down as much of him as I can. His head falls back against the couch as I take more and more of his shaft down my throat while running a hand up over his abs to his chest.

"Oh, god, baby, I'm going to come," he groans, trying to pull away.

I don't let him, and I don't stop. I want him to come. I want him to explode, and I want to taste him.

"Jenna!" He lets out tortured groan, trying again to pull away.

This time I double down and slide even more of him down my throat and swallow.

"Fuck, fuck, fuck," he grunts as his cum spills down my throat.

His hand goes to the back of my head and holds me there, but I'm not sure he realizes he's doing it. He lets go when he finally relaxes.

Phoenix looks down at me and cups my cheek with a look that I'd almost say is full of love if I didn't know it was just the post sex haze.

"That was amazing, but I didn't want to c-ome, not yet." He places two fingers under my chin and pulls me up to kiss him.

"I know. That's why I asked if you trusted me. It takes the edge off." I slide back up his body, kissing over his abs and chest until he grips my hips and pulls me up to straddle his lap.

His hands glide over my body as if to memorize it, and he kisses me gently. There's no rushing, and he finally slips his hand between my legs, stroking me. The feeling is exquisite and I want more, much more. Now it's me wanting to hurry things along.

"You're so wet," he murmurs against my lips when his fingers reach my core.

"I always am around you." I kiss him again.

He plays with my breasts, leaving a trail of fire. When he tweaks my nipples, I cry out.

"You still want this?"

Looking him in the eye, I say, "More than I want my next breath."

Breathing heavily, he says, "Condoms are in my room..."

I place a finger over his lips. "I'm on birth control, the shot, and have been for years.

I've been checked and I'm clean if you don't want to..."

He doesn't move or speak.

"Just thought you should get the full experience your first time."

He pulls me down for a kiss, then grips my legs and pulls me to him. "You let me have you this way, and we'll never use condoms. You okay with that?" he whispers against my lips.

"Yes."

Lining myself up with him, we lock eyes before I slowly slide down his hard shaft. He fights to keep his eyes locked with mine, but once I'm fully seated on him, his eyes roll back and he grinds his teeth. I love watching him fight back his climax, and I wonder how long he can keep control.

I try to memorize every detail because it won't be like this again. He'll know what to expect next time, and the sensations won't be new. But I love his inexperience and wish it could be like this every time. Maybe we'll have to find new and exciting things to try together, which could be fun.

As I move up and down on him, his large cock fills me to the brim. Once again, his eyes are everywhere. On my breasts as they sway and jiggle, and where we're connected. His eyes are riveted on me as I slide down him and he disappears inside me. I feel free and powerful because the look on his face is pure exotica.

"Fuck, you feel like heaven," he says as he drags his eyes up to mine.

"I'll have...to agree you feel...the same way," I huff.

He gives me a shy half-smile before gripping my hips and digging his fingers in to change up the pace. Then he slows me down like he wants to make this last, and I can't blame him because I want that, too.

"You look so good taking my cock," he groans.

"Damn, you like to talk dirty, huh? You just got so much hotter."

My core tightens around him as I teeter on the edge of an intense orgasm.

"You like dirty talk?"

I don't get to answer because he switches his angle and steals my breath on his next thrust.

"What about those beautiful tits bouncing in my face? Are they sensitive?" he asks before latching on to one and finding out for himself that they are.

Digging my nails into his shoulders, I try to hold on. But when his thumb makes contact with my clit, it only takes a few strokes before I'm coming so hard my vision starts to close in on me.

Phoenix releases a groan and fills me with his cum.

Unable to hold up my own body, I collapse onto his chest and rest my head on his shoulder. "Was it how you thought it would be?" I ask breathlessly.

He smooths his hands up and down my back, still seated inside me. "No, I couldn't have imagined that. That was mind-blowing. When can we do that again?" he asks, already hardening inside me.

"Let's make it to the bedroom at least. It'll be more comfortable." I grin.

He stands with me in his arms and I lock my legs around his hips as he carries me to the bedroom. I have a feeling we won't be leaving any time soon.

CHAPTER 18

PHOENIX

Waking up with Jenna next to me for the first time is a memory I don't ever want to forget. She's still sleeping, so I take in every little detail—the way the sunlight hits her hair, and how the sheets have bunched around her waist, leaving her breasts in full view.

Even in her sleep, she seems to gravitate toward me. Taking this time, watching her, I know in my gut that I love this woman. She's amazing and thoughtful and beautiful and seems to fit into my life here. Better than I could have ever hoped.

I want her here in the cabin, and I want her to wake up next to me every morning. It's only been one morning, but after today I don't think I can handle sleeping in a bed without her. I'm addicted to her.

Taking advantage of her in my bed, I run a hand down her side and over her hip. She barely stirs, so I nudge her onto her back and spread her legs. The sight of her wet pussy, even in her sleep, turns me on. Not wanting to waste any time, I lick up her cream as I watch her to see when she starts to awaken. I suck on her clit as I insert two fingers inside her and lazily build her orgasm.

She begins to stir and shift her hips but fights to open her eyes like she doesn't want the dream to stop.

"Good morning, baby," I say before latching onto her clit.

Her eyes shoot open and land on me the moment her orgasm crashes into her. Her back bows off the bed and her fingers dig into my scalp. I love the pinch of pain, knowing it's because I'm giving her pleasure.

When her entire body tenses up and she screams my name, I don't slow down. I keep going, dragging out her orgasm as long as possible and licking up every drop she gives me before sliding back up beside her.

When she opens her eyes again, she gives me a lazy smile and tries to reach for me.

"This was all about you this morning." I kiss her and she melts back into the bed.

"Take your time getting up. I'm going to make you breakfast, and then we need to go into town." I force myself to get out of bed and head for the door before I change my mind and spend all day ravishing her.

"Where are we going?" Jenna asks once we're in my truck and heading down the mountain.

"First, we're going to your place so you can get a fresh set of clothes. Actually, I'd like for you to pack a bag. Then, we're going to meet the guys at the shop, and I know Emelie would like to see you again."

At her place, Jenna doesn't waste any time changing into new clothes and packing a bag.

"Bring your computer, phone charger, and anything you need to work. I have internet in the cabin that you can use," I tell her, taking the bag from her.

Turning, she packs a second bag and grabs a book from the coffee table. "Other than a few pieces of furniture, everything I own fits in my car. Too much more, and I'm going to be moving in with you."

I know she's joking, but I almost tell her to do it—grab all her stuff and I'll have someone bring her furniture up to the cabin and move her in.

But I have to remind myself to take it slow, especially since coming to Montana was all about her gaining her freedom.

The moment we walk into the shop, Emelie bounces right over to Jenna. As I unload some items for Jack, they start whispering.

"Jenna and I are going to walk down to the cafe so we can talk about you without you hearing us. We're going to get a couple of snacks, and then we'll be back," Emelie says casually like it's an everyday thing.

"Little One," Axel growls.

"What? It's only four buildings down. You can look out the front door and see us. We will be right back." Emelie tries to give him a stern look but the love between the two of them is evident.

Axel gives her a small nod, and she takes Jenna's hand as they rush out of the store. Jenna looks over her shoulder at me. I give her a small smile to reassure her that it's okay, even though I understand how Axel feels about not wanting to have the girls too far away.

"Seems like things are working out with the two of you," Bennett says.

"Yeah, things have gotten pretty serious over the last few days. She was at the cabin when the storm rolled in, so she's been staying with me."

Axel and Bennett give each other a look because that's exactly how Axel managed to win Emelie over. Only they were stuck in his cabin for over two weeks when the road from his place into town was washed out.

"Maybe you should try it, Bennett. It's worked out for Axel and me so far," I smirk at him. He just grunts.

Bennett and Cash may not admit they want what Axel and Emelie have, but they do. Just like I do.

"How is Cash doing?" Jack changes the subject.

"The same. Last time I talked with him, he was exhausted. He was overjoyed at Emelie's food. I guess his brother did most of the cooking, so he's learning to take care of himself for the first time," I tell them.

"I'll have my Little One make some more casseroles for him. She feeds me, too, when she cooks for him." Axel smirks, and I know there's more to the story.

We chat for a few minutes until Emelie and Jenna return, each holding paper bags from the café. Emelie walks right to Axel with a big smile on her face, and the moment she's in his arms, he relaxes.

I know that feeling because the moment Jenna is at my side, and I can wrap an arm around her waist, I relax as well.

What I don't expect is for her to lean in and whisper in my ear. "Take me to the cabin, Phoenix."

Her words instantly have me hard, and my brain doesn't function for a moment.

"Time to go," I say, clearing my throat.

I hear the guys snicker as we leave. I don't care what they think. If my girl wants to go home, then we go home.

Once Jenna is secured in her seat and we're on the way home, she reaches for my hand.

"What's in the bag?" I ask.

"A surprise."

"Did you have a good chat with Emelie?"

"The best. I like Emelie. I don't think I've ever had a true friend like her. Even though

I've known her for such a small amount of time, she's the best friend I've ever had."

I know the feeling. It's how I felt coming here and meeting Jack and Bennett, and later Cash and Axel. My first real friends who didn't care about money or where I came from, they just cared about me, quirks and all.

"I'm glad you have her, and it's only a matter of time before Cash and Bennett meet someone and our circle grows even more."

She gives me a blinding smile. "It would be great to see both of them happy. We could meet up at the store, and us girls could have lunch at the cafe once a month. Then later..." She trails off.

My mind goes to later when we all have kids running around. I can see it so clearly, and I want it more than anything. But I just have to be patient and not push her too hard.

"Why are you going so slowly?" Jenna asks as I pull over to let a car go around us up the mountain.

"The roads are still wet and it's too easy to spin out or lose control of the car," I tell her.

As if the universe wants to prove a point, a small sports car with California plates whips around the corner going toward town and loses control. It spins out and hits the side of the mountain, ending up in the ditch.

"Holy shit!" Jenna gasps, visibly shaken.

"Stay in here. Lock the doors. I'll go check on them. Have service on your phone?"

Jenna checks her phone. "Yes."

"Call 911 and tell them we're just north of the 141 crossing on Whiskey Mountain Road."

She starts dialing, and I carefully make my way to the little car that got lucky, ending up in the ditch instead of going over the edge of the mountain.

Peeking in the window, I see a kid who can't be more than nineteen. He was probably showing off for the girl in the passenger seat who looks even younger than him. Both are awake, albeit stunned.

When I knock on the window, they look at me wide-eyed, but he's able to roll the window down.

"You two, okay?"

"I think so," the guy says, looking over at the girl who nods.

"My girl just called for help, but this is a dangerous curve. If you can move, you should come wait by my truck."

They're both slow at unbuckling and getting out before following me back to my truck. I open the tailgate so they can sit on it. They both have a few scratches but otherwise, look okay. The car might not be so lucky since it hit the side of the mountain after landing in the ditch.

"Thank you for stopping," the girl says.

Nodding, I watch Jenna in the car. She turns to look at me through the back window and gives me a thumbs up.

The two kids don't speak again until the paramedics and police get here. Jenna and I give our report of what happened, and an hour later, we're finally on our way home.

Neither of us says anything, but the moment we're in the cabin I pull Jenna into my arms.

"I'm okay, Phoenix," she says against my chest, holding me tight.

"I'm not letting you go, just the same."

"Let me put my stuff away, and then you can hold me until dinner. I promise."

Only then do I let her go and collapse on the couch. This life isn't for everyone, and I wonder what the final straw will be to send her running.

CHAPTER 19

EMELIE

I can't wait to get to the store today to see Jenna. I have a plan, and I'm not sure how Axel will take it, so I haven't shared it with him. He's less likely to say no in front of the guys.

"What's wrong, Little One? You're bouncing in your seat worse than a kid at Christmas."

It's funny that he's picking up on some of the phrases I say all the time and, for a moment, I almost forget why I'm nervous.

"I'm excited to see Jenna. Just like you need your time with the guys, I need my time with other girls." I lean over and kiss his cheek, and he wraps an arm over my shoulder, holding me to his side the rest of the way there.

We're the first ones at the store, so I focus my energy on bringing in our deer jerky and helping Jack organize and label it. When Bennett shows up, I help with his stuff while they talk.

When I'm done, I walk to Axel's side, and he pulls me to him as he talks with the guys. Finally, Phoenix and Jenna show up.

Jenna's eyes go right to me, and I know there's something she wants to talk to me about.

I beeline right to her and hug her. "I need to talk to you, but not around the guys."

"The cafe down the street?" she whispers.

"We can try."

Taking a deep breath, I turn back to the guys. "Jenna and I are going to walk down to the cafe so that we can talk about you without you hearing us. We're going to get a couple of snacks, and then we'll be back."

My voice doesn't even shake, but Axel's eyes never leave me.

"Little One," Axel growls.

"What? It's only four buildings down. You can look out the front door and see us. Don't worry, we'll be right back." I try to look serious as Axel's eyes zero in on me. Though I can tell he's at war with himself about letting me have freedom and keeping me safe.

Axel gives me a small nod, and I take Jenna's hand and pull her out of the store before he has a chance to change his mind.

Once outside, I take a deep breath of fresh mountain air and loop my arm through Jenna's. "I love walking Main Street," I tell her as we stroll past a few stores to get to the Cafe.

Walking this way, we're facing the mountains as they loom over the town. The view is nothing short of breathtaking.

"This view caused me to fall in love with this town," Jenna says.

"Yeah, it sealed the deal for me, too. I was already in love with Axel by the time I saw this view the first time, but that's when I knew there was nowhere else I'd rather be."

When we get to the cafe, we take our time looking over the display case at all the sweet treats inside. It's hard having to choose because I want to eat all of it. There are a few small birthday cakes, which remind me. "Phoenix's birthday is tomorrow, but he hates to celebrate it. I'm not sure why, so maybe don't make a huge deal about it." I tell Jenna.

Her eyes go dark. I'm guessing Phoenix has shared with her why he doesn't like birthdays. I'm glad he's opening up to someone.

"I'll get him a cupcake and do something small at the cabin," she says as we place our order for some fudge and her cupcake.

We grab a seat outside, sitting on the same side to take in the views as we eat fudge.

"He told you why he hates his birthdays, didn't he?" I ask hesitantly.

"Yes, he told me what happened."

"Good. He needs to talk to someone. I'm glad he has you. Things are going well?"

"Yeah. He just had me pick up some clothes to take to his place. It's like he doesn't want me to leave. Might have something to do with this time of year, too." She shrugs and while I want to know more, I don't think it's my place to pry.

"So, I looked into having a baby out here, and then Axel caught me. He thought I was pregnant, and the hope in his eyes…" I trail off, remembering that moment just a few days ago.

Jenna wraps her arm around me.

"But I'm not pregnant, and telling him was like watching his heart break right in front of me. We started talking, and he wants a home birth in our cabin. Everything I'm reading about it is super scary." I whisper the last part.

"I haven't thought about kids out here. But now that I am, it is a bit scary," Jenna says.

"Especially when you have no idea what to expect," I admit. "Axel made it clear he wants kids as soon as possible. We've been married for a year now, so I'm shocked he hasn't managed to knock me up yet. But I want to hold off and give us time together, just us."

"Then you have to tell him. But wrap it in love. Tell him how much you love him and want a little more time before you have to share him. That man will give you anything you want," Jenna says.

"So will yours." I giggle as we stand up.

Jenna grabs her bag with the cupcake and we go back to the store. We walk slowly, not wanting our girl time to end. Yet when we walk back into the store, I hurry right to Axel. All of a sudden, it's like I can't stand to be away from him a moment longer.

The moment his arms are around me, he relaxes, and so do I.

"Take me home, My Giant." I nuzzle into him.

It's time we talk, and maybe keep practicing this baby-making thing.

Chapter 20

Jenna

While Emelie and I were walking to the cafe in town yesterday she let it slip that today is Phoenix's birthday. But he doesn't like to celebrate it and knowing what I do about his parents, I can understand why. Yet I wasn't going to let the day pass without some form of celebration, which is why I came back with the bag he asked about.

Today I plan to do a little something for him and try to make some good memories. My idea is to spoil him rotten with food and orgasms.

I'm awake before him and watching him sleep. It's hard to tear myself out of bed, but I do it anyway, grabbing the cupcake I bought and placing the candle in it. I light it and gingerly walk back to the bedroom.

Climbing up on the bed, I carefully move to him on my knees. Thankfully, that motion wakes him up, but when he opens his eyes and sees the candle, his whole face falls.

I refuse to let the day be about sad memories because today we're going to make some good ones. "I understand why you don't want to celebrate your birthday, and I get what this date means, but I refuse to let you continue to mourn on your birthday. So I'm going to start filling it with good memories. And that starts now. Happy birthday! Close your eyes and make a wish."

For a minute he doesn't move, just stares at the cupcake like his mind is elsewhere.

I move closer to him and the fog clears. He sits up, saying nothing as he looks between me and the cupcake. It's like there's something that he wants to say, but he's debating whether he should. I wait, knowing there's a lot going on in his head he needs to work out today. It won't be an overnight process to turn today around, but this is a start, and I have to be patient with him.

Finally, he shakes his head like he's shaking away the bad thoughts. He forces a smile, closes his eyes, and blows out the candle.

I sit next to him on the bed and smile. I'm going to enjoy the next part even more than he is.

"Do I get to eat the cupcake?" he asks in a playful tone.

"Oh, yes. But the catch is you have to eat it off of me." I dip my finger in the frosting and run it between my breasts, then pull the shirt up to hide it.

He growls and a moment later he takes the cupcake from me. He sets it on the bed, and in the blink of an eye, my shirt is off, leaving me naked. Wanting to see what he does, I lay down, and he doesn't delay.

After licking up the frosting, he sucks on each of my nipples, causing an electric zing right to my pussy. Dipping his finger in the icing, he begins drawing his way down to my clit. He takes his time licking up every bit of frosting.

He drives me crazy, focusing on some places and ignoring others. I know he's doing it on purpose because of the wicked smile he gives me.

Taking his time, he eats every crumb of the cupcake off of me before he fucks me. I'm so damn turned on, and so is he, that while it doesn't last long, it's explosive. Then we shower together and spend the day making love all over the cabin.

• • • • ● • ● • • •

Phoenix's birthday was several days ago, and we've been taking it easy. While he works in the workshop, I work in the cabin, or sometimes out in the shop with him. What I really enjoy is helping him do the winter prep.

Yesterday, we picked a bunch of wild berries to make homemade jam and canned the rest. I looked up some pie recipes and made one for dessert that ended up being eaten in much the same way as his birthday cupcake.

Today we're going back into town to get some things from my cabin because I forgot the SD cards that have the photos I took before I moved here. They're still packed away in my closet. Plus, Phoenix asked me to bring some more clothes and even hinted about simply moving in all my stuff, but I brushed it off.

"Are you sure spending all this time with me isn't going to hurt your winter prepping?" I ask him, worried that I'm going to set him too far behind this year.

"I'll be fine. Plus, I always stock up at the store. If that means I have to buy more than I usually do, then so be it. I think it's worth the trade-off."

I know that isn't the most romantic line in the world, but it absolutely melts my heart. You'd have to know Phoenix and how these mountain men live to understand. They don't go to town to buy things from the store unless they absolutely have to. They prefer to live off the land. So the fact that

Phoenix is willing to make that sacrifice and depend a bit more on the store so that he can spend more time with me is huge.

"Does the mountain become impossible to navigate in the winter?" I ask because I've been thinking about what we'll do when the extreme weather arrives.

Will we just not see each other until spring? While I don't like that idea, I don't know if I'm ready to move in with him for several months straight.

But by now I should know that he picks up on what I'm thinking. Sometimes I think he can read my thoughts.

Leaning over, he takes my hand in his and brings it to his mouth, kissing my knuckles. "It does, and we have some time to figure it out. But so you know where I stand regarding winter, I plan on prepping enough for both of us because I want you up there with me. I don't think I'll be able to go several months without seeing you or being able to touch you."

When he runs his hands down my side and leans in to kiss my neck, it drives me crazy enough to make his point that I won't be able to go that long without him, either.

Just like that, he puts the ball in my court. He wants me there with him in his mountain cabin, and he's going to plan on having me there. I just have to make the jump and actually be there.

It's not something I have to decide right this moment as we still have a few months to go. A lot can happen in a few months, but if things keep going the way they have been, I'll definitely consider spending the winter with him on the mountain.

Walking into my house, everything is where I left it. As much as I used to look forward to coming back to my own place and snuggling up to read or watch TV, I don't anymore. What I look forward to is being with Phoenix in his cabin, with his arms around me. That feels like home now, so I decide to pack more than I need in my bag like he keeps asking me.

It takes me longer than I thought to find the older memory cards of the photos I took before I moved up here. When I finally start to pack my bag, Phoenix joins me in my room.

"Did you find what you needed?"

"I did. I was thinking of maybe packing a few extra clothes?"

He gives me one of those rare blinding smiles as he takes a few steps toward me and rests his hands on my hips. "Pack all your clothes, I have plenty of room."

"Slowly, Phoenix. Let's just take it slowly." I rest my hand on his chest and his heart beating under my hand is calming.

"As slow as you want, baby." He leans in and places a soft kiss on my lips. I want to take it further, but the knock on the door stops me.

I tense because the last time someone was at my door with Phoenix here, it was Chad. I'm beginning to hate people stopping by. Maybe I'm more like Phoenix than I realize. His no trespassing idea is looking better and better.

I sigh and step out of his arms to go see who is at the door. Immediately, I regret opening it.

"Mom! Dad! What the hell are you doing here?"

CHAPTER 21

PHOENIX

Jenna's parents are here.

From what I know, she didn't tell her parents where she was. I'm now wondering if the ex told them.

She seems as shocked as I am that they're here and tries to close the door on them. But her dad is faster and stops it with his foot.

"You've had your fun rebellion, Jenna. It's time to come home," her dad says.

"This isn't a rebellion. This is my life. A life away from you. A life I want," she fires back.

Her parents push their way inside and take a look around. The place is still pretty empty, mostly because she's been spending so much time with me. She has some bar stools at the kitchen island, but I'm still working on her table. There's a couch, a coffee table, a TV, a bed in her bedroom, and that's it. There's very little on the walls, and the place doesn't look lived in.

"This is where you live?" her father asks in disgust.

"Sweetheart, you can't live like this. You're in the middle of nowhere, and there's nothing in this town," her mom says.

I'd hate to see what they think of my place, which really *is* in the middle of nowhere. Even with no furniture, this cabin is a lot fancier than mine.

"This place is mine and I'm taking my time to make it my home. So what?"

"Honey, it's time to come back. You've had your time to recover from what Chad did to you, and people are asking about you. Just the other day, Spencer MacIntosh was asking after you." Her mom smiles and gushes over the name, and I can tell she thinks this Spencer guy is a big deal.

Her father is looking around the place. When his eyes land on me, he jerks, almost like I hit him.

"Jenna, did you know there's a strange man in your house?" her father asks as if she had no idea I was here.

"Yes. This is Phoenix. We just stopped home for me to grab a few things, and then we were heading back out."

It doesn't escape me that Jenna doesn't introduce me as her boyfriend or even her friend, just by my name. I try not to read too much into it, but it stings because I see her as my girlfriend, and if I'm honest, as so much more.

But she was never meant to be here, was she?

"Phoenix, why are you in my daughter's house?" her father asks.

I open my mouth, unsure what to say.

Jenna beats me to it. "He's here because I asked him to be. But I did not ask the two of you to come here, so it's time to go. I'm sorry you wasted your time."

"Just because you paid Chad back for the wedding doesn't make living like this okay," her mom says.

I can feel the blood draining from my face. Shit. Jenna wasn't supposed to find out like this.

"What are you talking about? I didn't pay Chad back that money. In fact, I made it very clear I wasn't going to," she says, looking as confused as her parents.

The more she stands there with her parents, the more I realize how much she doesn't fit in here. I was fooling myself, thinking she was learning how I live for anything but her book.

"Come on, let's move you into the pool house. It will give you the privacy you want, but you'll still be close. You can attend the Children's Hospital Gala and reenter society. We can find you a great catch there."

"Get out!" Jenna snaps.

Her mom jerks back like Jenna slapped her instead of just yelling at her. "Jenna–"

"No. This is my place! Get out or I'll call the cops on you for trespassing. Then I'll make sure all your friends back home see those photos," Jenna says as she opens the door.

"Well, I never!" Her mom storms out.

"That makes two of us," Jenna says.

"This isn't over," her dad says, following her mother.

Jenna closes the door and locks it. She stares at the closed door for a moment before she turns back to me. "I didn't pay Chad that money."

I swallow. "I know. I did."

She stares at me in disbelief. "Why? Why would you do that?"

"I didn't want him bothering you anymore. I didn't like him harassing you, so I took care of it."

"Without talking to me."

"Would you have let me do it if I had?" I ask, already knowing the answer.

"No, of course not. It was my issue to deal with, and I wasn't paying him back for the wedding. He's money hungry, so the last thing I was going to do was give him any. And that was my choice to make."

"I should've told you. I'm sorry, but all I want to do is protect you. From the moment I saw you in the shop, when you got that call. I knew someone was bothering you. I saw it on your face, and I wanted to protect you even then."

"But this was still my choice to make. I can't have you interfering in big things like this without talking to me."

Neither of us says anything. We just stare at each other, waiting for the other to speak.

"Maybe you should go back with your parents. We both know this won't work out. You're too city, and you won't survive a winter here, even in town. We're too different, and you don't fit in here."

"What the hell are you talking about?"

"Jenna, finish your book and go home to your family. At least you have one. No matter how horrible you think they are, it's better than not having one."

I move around her toward the door, thinking she'll let me go.

"Well, I guess you got what you wanted. Pay off my debt, fuck me, and send me away. So much for being different. Thank you for making me feel like a whore."

When she slams the door behind me, I jump.

She is the furthest thing from a whore, and I never saw her that way. I want to yell through the door and tell her that, make sure she understands it. But what is there I can say now that will make her hurt any less?

Slowly, I make the drive home. I expected to have her at my side, but now with an empty passenger seat, my heart is breaking.

I walk into my cabin, instantly feeling her presence. Her computer is still on the kitchen island, and I know if I walk into the bedroom, her clothes will be there, her stuff mixed with mine in the bathroom.

Even though I know I have to get everything back to her, I can't bear to see her right now.

Going to the radio I do the only thing I can think of.

"Emelie, you there? I need a favor."

CHAPTER 22

JENNA

I stare at the closed door in shock. What the hell just happened? Not twenty minutes ago, Phoenix was telling me to pack more clothes and was happy to go as slow as I wanted. Now, he's telling me to go home to the parents he knows I was running away from.

I don't know how long I stand there and stare at the door, but I only move to sit on the couch when my legs start to hurt. That's when the tears start, and I can't get them to stop.

Getting up, I try to find something to eat, but the thought of taking a single bite has my stomach rolling. Instead, I go take a shower and get ready for bed, hoping the water will soothe me. But in the end all it does is remind me of taking a shower with Phoenix, and that starts the tears all over again.

My mind tries to digest everything that happened. I've been focusing on him leaving and pushing me away, but now the focus is on the money.

He paid Chad back even after I said I wasn't going to do so. After everything, he gave Chad the money.

Why would he do that?

The words I said to him come back to me. I was hurt and was trying to wound him but, in reality, I do feel like it's the truth. Or, at least, some obscure version of the truth.

Before the sun sets, I lay down in bed and I cry myself to sleep.

When I wake the next morning, I have a headache, and I don't want to get out of bed. My eyes are red and puffy, but for the first time since Phoenix walked out the door, I'm hungry.

Grabbing some cereal without milk, since it's expired, I sit down to eat dry crunchy cereal and think about what the hell I'm going to do next.

The more I think about what Phoenix said yesterday, the more I wonder if he's right. I'm lucky enough to still have both my parents. Maybe I felt trapped in the marriage with Chad, and things weren't as bad as I remember.

Now Chad is marrying someone else, maybe things will be better. By the time I finish the bowl of cereal, I've talked myself into going home for a visit to get my head on straight. I need to figure out how to get my stuff I left at Phoenix's without having to face him.

As if the universe is reading my mind, there's a knock on the door. I freeze, not wanting to move an inch.

"Jenna, it's Emelie!" she calls through the door.

I rush to open it and let her in.

"Phoenix told me you had a fight and asked me to bring you the stuff you left at his place."

"A fight is an understatement," I sigh.

"Want to talk about it?" she asks.

"Yeah, I think I could use another opinion."

Emelie looks over her shoulder, and Axel shuts off his truck before making his way into the house. We sit on the couch, me on one end, Axel on the other with Emelie on his lap. Just seeing how much he loves her has tears filling my eyes again despite thinking I didn't have any more in me.

I tell them what happened yesterday. From how Phoenix and I were in a good place, my parents showing up, Phoenix leaving, right up to my thoughts this morning.

Emelie and Axel look at each other before Emelie starts talking.

"Neither of us has our parents in our lives anymore, so I understand his perspective, but I don't think your view was clouded.

Just because you have parents doesn't mean you have good parents. Bad parents can be worse than no parents at all because that relationship can be toxic, but you feel like you can't leave them."

"Phoenix sees this life he wants you to be a part of but you come from society and want to give it all up for harsh winters in his cabin. He's doubting it," Axel says. "With Emelie, I doubted it all the time until she showed me that first winter she could handle it."

"Of course, by then we were married," Emelie adds. "And I wasn't leaving no matter what." They smile at each other before Emelie turns back to me. "Phoenix wants to make sure you have no doubts. I can tell you that man is head over heels for you. He looks at you the way Axel looks at me. That said, if you go back to him, make sure it's for good. Now's the time to get rid of any doubt because if you go back and change your mind later, it will crush him."

"If he even wants me back."

"He wants you back. He wanted you back before he even pulled out of your driveway," Axel says.

It makes me wonder what Phoenix said to them.

"Well, I'm going to go home and visit my parents. I doubt they've changed, but I need to know for sure. Plus, it would be good to show my face now that everything has calmed down." I tell them my plans, so at least someone knows where I am.

· · · ● · ● · ● · ·

Driving into Denver doesn't give me those coming home vibes you see on that popular movie channel. I'm not excited to see old friends. In fact, I'm dreading it. I'm not smiling about fond childhood memories as I drive down the street I grew up on. I'm just tired and anxious.

This morning, I called my mom, telling her was coming for a visit, and asked to stay in the pool house. She said she'd have it ready for me. Even though I stressed this was a visit, she started making all sorts of plans, including going to the Children's Hospital charity gala in a few days.

I didn't get a chance to say no, and by the time I hung up, I figured maybe it would be a good way to show my face. Who knows, things might be different now?

When I pass through the gate, I don't stop at the main house, going straight to the back and parking by the pool house. I'm carrying my bags into the house when the man who I presume is my parent's newest butler arrives to help me. He leaves the moment my bags are in the pool house, and I sit down to look around. The place hasn't changed much since I was in high school when I'd sneak out here to get a break from my parents.

My peace and quiet is broken when my mom walks in without knocking. "Why didn't you stop at the main house, dear? We've been waiting for you."

"Because I wanted to get my stuff out of the car and stretch a bit."

My mother looks at me because my tone is short and clipped—nothing like the daughter who used to try so hard to please them.

Get used to it, Mom. This is the new improved me.

She goes on to talk about who's doing what, and who's engaged as if I care about any of these people. To be honest, I couldn't pick half these people out of a lineup. When I stand and begin to unpack, she follows me and keeps talking.

"So, the day after tomorrow, I have a spa day planned for us before the gala. You need your hair cut, and you're in desperate need of a facial, so we'll get that all taken care of. Also, I'm having several dresses delivered for you to choose from to wear at the gala. I'll have the rest sent back."

"Okay, Mom. I'm going for a swim. I've been in the car for the last two days, and would love to stretch my legs." Desperate to get away from her, I make up an excuse.

"Of course. Make sure you aren't late for dinner. Your father is leaving the office early to have dinner with you."

"I'll be there," I say, managing to keep my groan to myself. The last thing I want is to dress up for a formal dinner, but that's all my parents know how to do. Formal dinners, dressed up, hair and makeup done.

Over the next few days, it's like I never left. My mom packs my schedule and has me up early and out late. She doesn't leave my side or allow me any free time. We're so busy, and she wants to fill me in on everything I need to know for our next event.

At night, all I can think about is Phoenix. I dream of our days together, about what winter with him would be like.

The night before the gala, I wake up in a cold sweat. One thing is crystal clear. *I hate everything about this life.*

Chapter 23

Jenna

I've spent the last three hours having my nails, hair, and makeup done for the gala. When the dresses showed up, my mom made me try on every one of them, and I let her pick. She chose an emerald green dress that shows off my curves and will look great on the dance floor, according to her.

Then my mom insisted I arrive in a separate car so my photos wouldn't be mixed in with theirs. If I wanted to stay later to talk to my friends, I'd have my own car. Again, her words not mine.

A long time ago, I learned it was easier to agree with my mother instead of trying to fight her on things. Especially anything that has to do with appearances, and I know this night is important to her.

I watch them arrive in the car in front of me. My father turns to her and helps my mom out of the car. They both smile for the cameras and the press goes crazy snapping photos of them.

When their car pulls away and mine pulls up, I know the drill. My driver waits until Mom and Dad are halfway up the walkway before opening my door. I step out, the camera's flash, and everyone yells out questions. Smiling and posing, I turn and join my parents who are smiling like we're this perfect American family.

Once inside, Mom grips my arm and steers me right over to Spencer Macintosh. "Look who got back into town earlier this week," she says to Spencer and his parents.

"I heard you were back in town, Jenna, and was hoping you'd be here," Spencer says.

I went to kindergarten with this man, and I can honestly say he peaked in middle school. He was a cute kid, but once puberty hit, it wasn't kind to him. He's tall, skinny, and pale with a little acne. He has the confidence of a player, though, and I'm guessing the only reason he gets any action is because of his family name and bank account.

"Yes, I'm in town visiting my parents," I tell him as my mom floats away to talk to someone else. I knew this was a setup.

"Oh, I heard you'd moved back from, where was it? *Montana*?" he asks, making "Montana" sound like a dirty word. I guess in his world it is.

"Well, you heard wrong. I'm just visiting and happened to be in town for the gala, so here I am." I smile to be polite, but when his eyes start running over my body, it feels gross and wrong.

It's not like when Phoenix's eyes run over me. That heats my body and turns me on like nothing else can. Spencer's eyes on me make me feel uncomfortable and violated.

"Well, maybe I can give you an incentive to stay?" he asks, but there's a cocky smirk on his face that says it's not really a question.

"I doubt it. Honestly, I'm enjoying being out of the city and away from all this. I've got a book deal I've been working on."

"That makes sense while you're in *Montana*. How long before you finish up the book and come home?"

I don't know why I'm irritated that he thinks I'm only there to do the book. Maybe it's the way he again made Montana sound like a dirty word. Or maybe it's because he's not understanding I'm done with this life.

That's when it hits me full force. I'm done with smiling for the camera and putting on the perfect face. I'm done with galas and charity events and fundraisers and fancy dresses. I'm done with spending hours on hair, makeup, and nails just to look perfect for a few hours at an event.

Hell, I'm done with the big city and the noise that fills the air at night. I'm done with not being able to see the stars from my front porch, and I'm done with all of these people.

But I gave my word to my mother about tonight, so while I may have to grin and bear it, I don't have to stand here with Spencer.

"Well, I guess I'll see where it takes me." I smile and head directly to the bar to get a drink.

The best part about my mom insisting I have a driver is that I can have a drink to make dealing with tonight easier. Though, I've also learned that at events like this, one glass of wine is my limit. It will relax me, but not make me tipsy as I need to have my words and wits about me to deal with the men in this room.

I don't even make it to the bar before I'm stopped by another man my mom has tried to set me up with in the past. I have no idea what his name is. I just remember he had a horrible sense of humor that bordered on racist. He talks to me like we're best friends. When he tries to tell me about the contract he's working on with my father, I finally put my foot down.

"It's funny because the last time my father talked about you, he said he wouldn't work with you even if it meant his business going bankrupt." Then I turn around and walk off.

Once at the bar, I place my drink order. While I'm waiting, another gentleman next to me turns around and grabs my butt as he smiles at me. I have no idea who this guy is. He's old enough to be my father and makes no effort to hide what he just did.

"That dress is the perfect choice for you," he says with a creepy smile.

"Touch me again, and not only will I break your hand, but I will also dislocate your dick." I smile at him as I take my wine from the bartender who's trying not to laugh, having overheard what I just said.

Now that I have a glass of wine in my hand, I move off to the side of the bar. I scan the room, looking for the best place to hide out until dinner. Unfortunately, right in front of me, stands Chad.

"I didn't think I'd see you at another of these events. But I'm glad you had the guts to show your face," he says without even the hint of a smile.

"Why should I be embarrassed to show my face? I wasn't the one who had to pay the newspapers to spin the fact that you jumped from one bride to the next." I say, giving him what I hope is an evil smile.

Over his shoulder, I see my mom notice who I'm talking to. Her eyes go wide and she excuses herself, picking her way over to me as fast as she can.

"If I'm being honest, Chad, I have to thank you."

Confusion fills his face. "Thank me for what?"

"If you hadn't made it so blatantly clear that you were only marrying me for the money, I would have married you that day. We would be married and miserable right now. But instead, I've been given a chance to be happy, to do something that gives me joy, and I never would have taken that leap if it hadn't been for you."

My mother stops not too far away, ready to jump if it looks like the situation is getting out of control.

Chad's eyes turn soft, and I see a hint of the man I first dated. The one I thought I was marrying.

"I've only ever wanted you to be happy, Jenna. Despite how our relationship started and how our marriage would have begun, I would've always made sure you were happy," he says in a soft tone.

I can feel the emotion behind it, and at that moment, I believe him, regardless of everything that's happened.

I don't get to reply because his new fianceé walks up, and his entire demeanor changes.

"Well, congratulations to you both." I smile and turn to walk away before either of them can say anything else.

I smile at my mother as I walk past her, and I do the same as I walk past my father. I'm sure they think I'm just making my way to the restroom, but they'll soon discover I'm not.

I text the driver to come pick me up. When I get to the side door away from all the press, he's there waiting on me.

"Is everything okay, miss?" the driver asks once we're heading back to my parents' house.

"Yes. I just realized this isn't where I'm supposed to be."

The driver gives me a big smile and there's a twinkle in his eye, like he knew all along what it's taken me until now to realize.

As soon as he drops me off at the pool house, I'm inside and changing out of the dress. I lay it on the bed so it's there when my mother finds it. Then I remove my makeup but leave my hair since it's curled and done up. If I tackle it now, it'll take me forever to brush it out.

Quickly, I pack my bags, and when I step out to start loading them in my car, the driver is there with a smile on his face.

"I'll load these for you, and then I'll go back to the gala. I'll inform your parents that you weren't feeling good, so you came home early and planned to go to bed. They won't know you've gone until morning."

"Thank you. I'm not sure why you're helping me out, but thank you." I don't know this driver. He's only recently begun working with my parents and this is the first time I've ever seen him.

"It may not make a lot of sense to you, but you went to school with my son. He was in school with you on a scholarship and wasn't popular. He had a huge crush on you because you were one of the only people that were truly nice to him. So, consider this my way of paying it forward."

I wrack my brain trying to think who his son is, and then it hits me. "Your son was Ethan Kirby."

"Yes, and getting that scholarship was a blessing to my family. But I know that going to school was hard for him, and he would always focus on you. How you made it worthwhile for him to go to school every day."

"Ethan was one of the kids that were nice for no reason. Until I met him, I hadn't known someone could be like that. My mom always packed these ridiculously healthy lunches with food I could never pronounce, and I was jealous that he would get peanut butter and jelly sandwiches and brownies and chips in his lunch. I'll never forget the day I sat down next to him. It was the middle of ninth grade and I was having a horrible day. His mom had sent him in with brownies and he gave me his brownie to make my day better. It was the first time I'd ever had a brownie, and from that day on, I felt protective of him."

"You know, I remember that day. He came home flabbergasted that someone his age had never eaten a brownie before. We talked about how he was in an entirely new world, and how he needed to tread lightly."

"I never knew he had a crush on me. But I always considered him a friend, and I wish he would have asked me out to homecoming or prom. I would have said yes," I say with a smile, remembering those moments hiding from the rest of the kids during lunch just for a bit of peace and quiet with him. "How is he now?"

"Well, he busted his butt, got into Yale, and then he worked even harder and ended up at Yale law school. After graduating early and working at a firm here in Denver for a year, he decided he needed a change. What he wanted was to do good versus make a lot of money, so he does pro bono and charity work now."

My mind immediately flips to Cash and how he's going to need someone he trusts on his side when his brother passes away.

"What type of work does he do?"

"A lot of family planning and estate planning, child custody, divorces, and criminal law when he sees someone is wrongly accused."

"And he's here in Denver?"

"Yes. Is everything okay?"

"My friend's brother is really sick, and he's not going to be around much longer. He's going to need someone he can trust to guide him on the right path. He's in Montana, and I know Ethan can't represent him there, but I would feel better having someone look over the paperwork before anything is signed. If I gave you a letter, would you give it to him?"

"I'd be happy to."

After placing the rest of my bags by the front door, Mr. Kirby loads them into my car while I pull out a notepad from the kitchen area. I write a quick letter to Ethan, telling him that I hate that we lost touch. Then I give him my number, letting him know I'm going back to Montana, but would love to reconnect and maybe talk to him about looking over some paperwork for a friend of mine.

I give it to Mr. Kirby, who then pulls me in for a hug before opening my car door and helping me in.

As I drive north and see the Denver city lights behind me, I smile, feeling at peace with my decision.

After driving for a few hours, I get to a hotel just outside of Casper, Wyoming. I still have a full day's drive to get back to Whiskey River. Only once I hit the Montana State line do all my doubts start to hit me, but there's only one question that keeps running through my head over and over.

Why didn't Phoenix want me?

CHAPTER 24

EMELIE

"I don't think this is a good idea, Little One," Axel says from beside me.

He's driving me to Phoenix's house. We were just there picking up Jenna's things from him and taking them to her. It was the first time I've been at Phoenix's house and seen his workshop. He didn't give me much time to look around because he wanted Jenna's things gone.

After stewing on what she said for the last few days, I decided I wanted to talk to Phoenix. Anyone can see the love they have for each other, but they're getting in their own way.

"You've said that several times now, and it's duly noted, but I have to do this. I have to try."

"I know you do, and that's why I haven't stopped you. I want them to be happy, too. Jenna is good for him, and I like you having another girlfriend out here to talk to."

"You can lead a horse to water, but you can't force him to drink," I sigh.

"What?" Axel asks, giving me his adorable, slightly confused look that makes me giggle.

"It means I'm only giving him advice. I can't force him to take it or do anything about it. He has to want to do that himself."

Axel squeezes my hand. It's always a treat driving here in the mountains. They're so beautiful, and there are many spots where the trees open up into breathtaking views. I hope I never take this place for granted.

As we start up Phoenix's driveway, I suddenly get nervous. These men are private people and don't like visitors. I did tell him via the radio I was going to stop by, but that doesn't necessarily mean he wants me here. Since I'm not sure how this will go, I'm glad to have Axel at my side. My Giant. I've never felt as safe as I do with him, and I know he won't let anyone hurt me, even his friends.

When we park at Phoenix's cabin, I step out of the car to the sound of an electric saw filling the air. He must be in his workshop. Axel walks over to me, taking my hand as we make our way over to where the noise is coming from.

Even though we don't say a word as we step into the large garage, Phoenix stops what he's doing and turns off the saw. He doesn't move at first, but when he turns to look at us, the dark circles under his eyes are evident and I know I made the right choice in coming to speak to him.

"Can we talk?" As much as I know I'm doing the right thing, he can still turn us away, and I'd respect that decision. If I push him too far, it won't do any good for anyone.

"Yeah. Let me clean up. We can talk inside," he says as we follow him into his cabin.

Axel sits on the couch in the living room facing the fireplace and pulls me onto his lap. He's been doing this more and more since we got married. It's like sitting next to him is just too far away. I don't complain because I like it, too. With his strong arms around me I feel safe, and it gives me the confidence I need to do things like this.

When Phoenix joins us, his steps falter at seeing Axel and me together. He takes a seat in the chair next to us and looks at me, waiting for me to speak.

"I took Jenna's stuff to her. But I have to say, she looked as miserable as you do now. She told us what happened, at least, what she wanted to tell us, but I know there's always more on a deeper level."

Phoenix grunts, but doesn't stop me from talking.

"I get that you aren't sure she'll be happy here. I know Axel had the same fears. Hell, every once in a while, I can still see that fear creeping in. The only way you'll ever know for sure is if you let her prove it to you. That means you have to stop pushing her away."

"She sees me as everything she was trying to get away from." His head falls to his hands as he rests his elbows on his knees.

"Did she say that?" I ask.

"No. She didn't have to."

"Maybe you should let her speak instead of assuming. Because I can tell you from talking with her, that's not how she feels at all."

He shakes his head but says nothing.

"Okay, well, if your goal was to push her away, goal accomplished. She went home. This is your turning point. It's going to take more than 'I'm sorry' to end this. Either fix it and be happy or spend the rest of your life up here alone. I'm willing to bet that doesn't sound as great as it used to."

I stand up and Axel follows me. I don't stop until I reach the front door when I turn back to look at him. "No matter what you choose, we're here for you. Anything you need, all you have to do is ask. Don't forget it."

On the way home, I doubt every word I said. Going back over everything, I try to figure out what I could have said differently to have made my point, and get no clear answer.

"He just needs time, Little One. Us mountain men can be a stubborn bunch," Axel says, trying to cheer me up.

"I know. I just hope he heard me because I don't think I can stand to see him like that for much longer. He deserves to be happy, to be loved. The kind of love you and I share."

"I got lucky when I met you. It's not every day someone meets the love of their life in a river in the middle of the mountains."

"No, that was fate leading me to My Giant, and I wouldn't have it any other way."

"Neither would I," he says, squeezing my hand.

"Now. Get me home and take me to the river."

CHAPTER 25

PHOENIX

I'm in the workshop, and everything Emelie said the other day keeps running through my head. It's been on a nonstop loop, and it doesn't matter if I'm awake or not. During the day I hear her words, and at night my dreams are filled with Jenna, who's happy back home in Denver and wants nothing to do with me.

One thing I can agree on is that I have to do something because spending my life alone on this mountain without her isn't an option. But have I fucked up too much to fix things? I told her to go home, and she did. I fully believe she should spend what time she can with her parents because she's lucky they're still around. Yet, how can I pull her away from them now?

I can't. Day after day, that's what has me frozen, trying to figure out my next move, and failing.

When I hear a car coming up the drive- way, I figure it's Emelie back to give me more wisdom that will keep me up at night. When I turn around and see Jenna's ex, Chad, I'm shocked. I don't know why I am. I gave him back the money he was demand- ing so, of course, he's back for more.

He looks over the workshop, clearly un- comfortable with being here before his eyes land on me.

"What are you doing here, Chad?" I walk to the doorway and stand there cleaning my hands on a rag. Instead of being covered in sawdust today like I was when Emelie came to visit, I've been working on a chair, so I have wood stain on my hands.

"You know Jenna is back in Denver?" he asks

My body stiffens. If he knows that, it means he's run into her. Are they going to get back together? I would hope after every-thing he's done that she wouldn't go there.

"Yeah, I heard," is all I give him, waiting to see what he says next.

He nods and takes a look around like he-'s uncomfortable in his surroundings and, out here, he should be.

"I ran into her the other night at a gala. It was evident her parents forced her to go. Her mom must have picked out the dress. You could tell it wasn't her style, and she just looked miserable. I realized that even back when we were together, she nev-er quite fit in. That night, it hit me hard."

"Okay?" I'm getting irritated. Is he just here to rub it in my face that he got to see Jenna, or that Jenna isn't with me anymore? I can't get a read on where this is going.

"We talked, and it was something we both needed. Once we got engaged, we stopped talking, and I think that was our downfall. After the engagement broke off, I let my parents get into my head, something Jenna always helped prevent. For a while, I was lost without her, but seeing her the other night was a wake-up call."

Chad pulls an envelope out of his back pocket and holds it up for me. Taking a few hesitant steps toward me, he holds the envelope out. I just stare at it, not wanting to accept it, especially since I have no idea what it is.

"I'm giving your money back. Again, I'm sorry I let my parents get into my head. It was easier to listen to them than to admit I failed and screwed all this up."

Hesitantly, I reach out and take the envelope. A quick glance shows it contains a stack of cash. I put the envelope in my back pocket because I don't care if it's all there or not.

"Anyway, I wanted to give that back to you and to tell you that you're a bloody idiot if you're going to let that girl go. She's miserable in Denver, she's unhappy without you, and if you don't get your ass together the next time I visit, you and I are going to have it out. I'll probably lose, but that's not going to stop me. Jenna and I were friends long before all this happened, and I just want her to be happy."

Because I have no idea what to say, I just nod. Chad stares at me for a moment longer before he goes back to his car. Just as he reaches it, another car pulls up the driveway.

I really need to add a gate and a lock. For someone who likes their privacy as I do, there are way too many people coming in and out lately. I moved to the mountain to get away from people, not to have a never-ending train of visitors.

Chad doesn't get in his car. He stares at the approaching vehicle. When I finally take my eyes off of him, I see that it's Jenna. Chad nods at her before getting into his car and driving off.

It's apparent this is going to be a shit show before the first word even comes out of her mouth. There's anger and irritation in her eyes, but I don't care. She's here, and regardless of how pissed off she is, I'm going to fix this.

"What the hell is Chad doing here?" she demands, her voice laced with anger.

I pull the envelope from my back pocket and hold it up for a moment before putting it back. "He came to give me back the money and to tell me that I'm an idiot. He threatened to harm me if I hurt you." I summarize Chad's visit.

Jenna's eyes go wide for a moment before she turns and looks at the cabin.

There are so many things I want to do. I want to go to her and pull her into my arms and hold her tight. I want to beg her to forgive me and come back. But she's here for a reason, and I have to know what that is.

"Jenna... " My voice breaks because I have no idea what to say to her.

When she finally turns back to me, her eyes are full of tears. That's when I see the dark circles under her eyes. Her hair is a mess, but she's still the most beautiful woman I've ever seen.

"Why didn't you love me?" she asks, her voice breaking.

I stand there in shock because it was never a fact of not loving her. I love her more than anything. It's why I wanted her to be happy, and I thought being happy meant her being in Denver.

Maybe Chad is right. I'm a bloody idiot, thinking that pushing her away would make her happy, even though it's impossible to think that she could be happy here with me. We all thought the same of Emelie when she met Axel, but she was meant to be out here on the mountain, so maybe Jenna is, too.

I stand there in shock for too long because Jenna continues before I can get a word out. "I hate the city. I hate the noise. I hate the people. I even hate my parents. My time there made me remember the reason I moved here, and it has nothing to do with you, and everything to do with me. I won't go back to Denver because that's not the life I want. It never was. You know that because I've told you."

She pauses and wipes away a few stray tears that have fallen down her face. I want nothing more than to pull her into my arms and wipe those tears away myself, but I'm frozen where I stand.

"I won't go back to Denver. If you don't want me, you need to be man enough to say it because I'm not going anywhere. You're going to have to deal with me in this town, so get over it."

Then she turns around to get back in her car.

CHAPTER 26

JENNA

I go to get in my car before my tears turn into a waterfall. After everything else, the last thing I need is for him to see me crying.

I'm just opening the door when his hand reaches around and closes it again. Then he presses his front to my back and whispers in my ear. "I do love you. So much so that it scares the hell out of me."

He turns me around to face him and pins my back to the car door as his lips land on mine. He cradles my face with one of his large, rough hands as his lips dance over mine. Softly at first, until I let out a moan. It seems to spur him on and he deepens the kiss, putting an end to any space between us.

I can feel how hard he is, and that alone makes me wet. Having his hands on me makes me even hotter, *but this kiss*. This kiss is on an entirely new level.

"I love you, Jenna, but I was so scared that you wouldn't want this life. You grew up so differently, I was just scared," he says against my lips, looking into my eyes.

"I love you, too, Phoenix. This is the life I want. I knew that before my parents showed up and I know it even more after my time in Denver. You have to trust me."

"I trust you. God, I trust you." He buries his head in my neck, and I wrap my arms around him, holding him to me.

He grips my ass and lifts me, so he doesn't have to bend down as far, but still keeps me pinned to the car as he kisses up my neck on his way back to my mouth.

When he rubs his stiff erection between my thighs, we both groan. I'm wearing a maxi dress and the thin fabric and my panties are the only thing separating me from him.

"I need you," I whisper against his lips, and he moans again.

He reaches his hand between us and pushes my dress up until his hand finds my core.

"Fuck, baby, you're soaked." He runs his fingers over my panties.

"I always am around you."

He pulls my panties to the side and dips his fingers through my folds before bringing them up to my clit. When he takes my nub and squeezes, I can't stop the mewl that comes from my mouth. He's driving me crazy.

"It's such a turn-on knowing I can do this to you. You have no idea." He punctuates his words with a thrust of his hips.

"No teasing, Phoenix, I need you so badly. It's been too long," I moan as he continues to play with my clit.

Just when I think I'm going to go insane without him, he rips my panties from me, dropping them on the ground. Then he opens his belt and his pants. He pulls his pants down just enough for his cock to spring out, and it bounces against my thigh. A second later, he's lined up at my entrance and his eyes lock with mine as he slowly slides into me.

It's only been a few days, but it feels like so much longer. Every inch he slides into me feels better than the one before. When he's fully seated in me, he steals my breath, gently kissing and holding me.

Then he deepens the kiss and slowly thrusts in the way he knows makes me burn. The scrape of his jeans on my inner thighs and the fact we still have most of our clothes on only makes this that much hotter. That we need each other so much we can't wait to get inside or remove our clothes makes it even hotter. Now that he's inside me again, I feel whole. I feel at home. The missing part of my soul is back, and I'm never letting it go again. This is where I belong. I know it without a shadow of a doubt, and in time, I'll prove it to my mountain man.

When he starts trailing kisses down my neck, he picks up the pace and his grip on my ass tightens. "You feel so fucking good baby. I missed you so damn much. I can't breathe without you," he says against my neck.

Before I get a chance to respond, he slams into me so hard that the slap of flesh echoes in the woods. "You are mine. Jenna."

"I'm yours, just like you're mine," I tell him.

"I've always been yours, even when I didn't know it was you I was waiting for," he says before reaching between us and rubbing my clit.

I'm already on the edge, so the little extra friction is enough to send my climax barreling into me. Arching my back, I scream out his name, and he keeps thrusting through my orgasm until his overtakes him. He buries himself deep inside me, whispering my name over and over again.

Basking in the glow of our orgasms, we stay locked in each other's arms for a moment. Then he sets me back on my feet and fixes my dress for me before taking care of himself.

When he bends down to pick up my ripped panties, he smiles. "These are mine." He shoves them into his pocket.

"What? Are you going to put them in the scrapbook we show our kids one day?" I joke, making him chuckle.

"Nope. They'll be my own private trophy."

We make our way into the cabin, and he pulls me onto his lap on the couch. He keeps running his hands over my arms and my back like he can't believe I'm here and he has to touch me to remind himself that I am.

"I'm sorry about what I said the last time we spoke. I was upset and in shock. You were the last person I expected to hurt me, and I guess I just wanted to hurt you back. I didn't mean it at all, and I am so sorry."

He softly brushes some hair from my face before cupping my cheek. "I know you didn't mean it, baby. I'm the one who should be sorry for not trusting you, for not trusting us. I was so scared that you would go back to that life once everything settled down, I pushed you away. I'm still terrified that after a winter here you won't want to stay, but I'm not pushing you away again."

I lean in and kiss him gently. "About Chad..." I start before he places a finger on my lips.

"I hated the thought that he had any kind of claim to you. Even if it was just trying to come at you for money. That's why I gave it to him. I wanted you to be free, but I know I should have told you, and I'm sorry."

"I saw Chad a few days ago. He seems... different. Happy, I guess. We had the closure I think we both needed. But seeing him here was the last thing I expected."

"You and me both. Though he did seem different. He apologized and told me he'd kick my ass if I hurt you, even though he admitted he knows he'd lose," he chuckles.

"Yeah, if his family didn't have money, he'd have been picked on horribly at school. He's always been smaller and awkward. But he bought protection from some of the bigger football players, and everyone left him alone." I laugh, but then become serious again. "No more secrets, Phoenix. I'm in this all the way, but we can't have any more secrets."

"I agree, baby. No more secrets and no more pushing you away. From now on, I'm holding on to you so tight."

I lean in for another kiss and my lips barely touch his before he's pulling back.

"In the light of no more secrets, I have to ask something."

My body tenses. While I have nothing to hide from him, I have no idea what he's going to ask. "Anything."

He leans in and places his lips next to my ear. His hot breath sends tingles down my spine. "How does it feel to have my cum coating your thighs?"

I gasp, and he takes that moment to pull me in for another kiss before carrying me to his bed, where he tells me he plans to keep me for the rest of the day.

CHAPTER 27

PHOENIX

After several rounds of lovemaking, Jenna passed out and I've been laying here holding her ever since. I still can't believe she's back, and that she chose me and wants me. I was prepared to go after her if she hadn't returned to me.

She chose to come back, and that means everything to me. I want her to know I don't take it lightly. I need her to know that I understand what it means to accept a life out here, and to show her I'm all in.

So I wait for her to wake up because she needs this nap. The drive here alone is two days, and who knows how long she's been back in town.

As I think of the future, I lightly run my hand through her hair, enjoying the silky feel of it. I know the moment she's awake because her whole body stiffens.

She opens her eyes, looks at me, and then smiles. "I was worried it was all a dream." She stretches, giving me an unobstructed view of her perky breasts.

"I'm still worried after the first winter here you'll bolt," I whisper.

She turns to look up at me and opens her mouth to speak, but I stop her. "Life out here isn't easy. As much as possible, I try to live off the land. If I have to buy something in town, I try to find a way to make it or do without it first. Just because I have money doesn't mean I use it. I live off of less than the interest in a savings account each month. My biggest expense is paying my yearly taxes on the land, and other than that, I don't spend any more than most people make in a month in the entire year."

"Phoenix, you know it's not about the money for me. If it was, don't you think I would have had a major shopping spree and decorated my cabin by now?" Jenna asks with a smirk on her face, trying to lighten the mood.

"I know money isn't a thing for you right now, and it may never be. But what about when winter hits and we can't even get down the driveway? When we're stuck on the mountain for months at a time and sometimes stuck inside for a week or more? Are you going to be able to handle it?"

"Do you know the kind of photos I can get on the mountain up here when we're snowed in? Even more than that, I can spend all of our time in the summer getting the photos I need as we prepare for winter, and spend all winter putting books together, editing photos, and doing all of my online work. I would love nothing more than long days curled up by the fireplace in the library reading with you. As long as it's with you. But above all else, I know I can do this because you have."

My heart starts racing because she's really thought this out, and I know I can't keep doubting her. I don't want to give her any reason to doubt me, so I reach into my nightstand and pull out the box that has been sitting there for a couple of weeks now, removing the ring inside.

I take her left hand and slide the ring on her finger. "Good. Because I want all of this with you, too. I want to marry you and do everything with you by my side. Hunting, fishing, winter prep, days in town, all of it, and more. Will you marry me?"

"Yes. A hundred times, yes." She grabs my face and pulls me down for a kiss. A kiss which pushes any doubt and fears I have aside, at least for now.

This kiss is a promise of the life I want.

· · • ● ● ● • · ·

Jenna

I've officially moved into Phoenix's cabin. After we spent a day in bed, he took me to go get all my stuff and demanded I bring everything but my furniture. I was happy to do it because I don't plan to spend any more nights away from him if I can help it.

I just unpacked the last box and put everything away, and I'm taking the boxes out to the workshop where we've been stacking cardboard. It took much longer than it should have because every time the light caught my ring I'd stop and stare at it, smiling and thinking of the future to come.

"Last box. Everything has a home." I smile at Phoenix.

"Good. You're stuck with me now."

I walk over and look at the table he's working on. My table. This is the one that was supposed to go in my dining room and be a showstopper in my cabin. This is the last thing I have to figure out before I finally feel settled. Phoenix says I have a few more weeks until he's done.

He's taking it slower than normal as he's been doing a lot of side work as well.

As a car pulls up the driveway, we both walk to stand in the large garage doorway.

"Must be Emelie and Axel. Emelie said she was going to make some more food for Cash," I say as we wait for the car to appear from the trees.

"That's not the sound of Axel's truck," Phoenix says hesitantly, and steps in front of me. I wonder if he did it on purpose, or if it was on instinct. Either way, I love that he wants to protect me.

A car pulls up with a dark tint and we wait for whoever's inside to step out. The last people I expect to see are my parents. They're dressed like they're going to a stockholder meeting in business formal. In short, they stick out like a sore thumb.

"Mom? Dad? What are you doing here?" I ask in shock, placing a hand on Phoenix's back to draw some strength from him.

"Well, you left with no warning, and just disappeared. Then you weren't in your house, so this was obviously the next place to look-," my father says in a bored tone.

"I told you I was only visiting. I never wanted to go to the gala, but you guys kept
pushing events on me and not listening. So,
there was no reason to stay."

"You can't live like... like... well, like this," my
mom says, looking around and not even
trying to hide the disgust on her face.

"Like what?" I want her to say it.

"No phone service," she says, flustered.

I want to laugh. Of course, that's what she's
worried about.

"That's what I love most about it. It's what
kept me coming back. But then I fell in love
with Phoenix, which was an added incentive."

"Well, we don't approve, and if you stay
here, we're cutting you off for good," my
father says, straightening his spine.

"You cut me off months ago, and I've been
fine. In fact, I prefer it."

That's when Phoenix finally makes a move.
He walks up to my father, who is a few
inches shorter than him. He holds out his

hand and smiles. "I don't think we've been properly introduced. I'm Phoenix March. I think you knew my parents, Thomas and Quinn."

Phoenix shakes my father's hand and at the mention of his parents' names, my mother's jaw drops, and my dad tenses.

When I was looking into his parents, I found out they were worth more than my parents by at least double. They had the kind of power to destroy my parents with a snap of their fingers, though, according to Phoenix they weren't like that.

"Well, you running off so recklessly makes sense now. Why didn't you just say you were shacking up with the March boy?" Dad laughs and shakes Phoenix's hand enthusiastically.

"Well, this is a turn of events. I approve. We'll have to clean you up, but I don't think I could have picked a better match myself," Mom says.

"Of course, you would. But regular old Phoenix, who makes your daughter happy and treats her like gold, isn't good enough.

So now it's time to turn the tables. I'm cutting you off." I glare at them and they both freeze.

"Oh, you don't mean that, darling. Your kids will need grandparents and connections for the best schools." Mom waves her hand.

"Phoenix has plenty of connections. We need nothing from you. The only thing I want is for you to disappear from my life. Do not step foot on our property again, or next time you will be greeted with a shotgun."

In a show of support, Phoenix wraps his arm around my waist, probably to keep me from lunging at them.

Maybe someday, I'll want to form a relationship with them. Perhaps in the future, they'll be part of our lives again, but right now we need this space and separation. It's my hope they'll change, but I'm okay if they don't. Our kids will have plenty of family here on the mountain between the guys and Jack.

We will build our own family.

CHAPTER 28

PHOENIX

Watching Jenna pick me is probably the greatest moment in my life. Life with me won't always be easy, and we've recently talked in depth about it.

Over the last few days, I've told her about how life was when I first moved out here and was learning to survive. Granted, it won't be that hard for her because she has me, and we have the guys for anything we don't know.

I introduced myself to her parents more as a "fuck you" than anything else. They thought I wasn't good enough for her. Well, newsflash, I feel the same way about them.

Anyone that treats this angel that way isn't good enough to share the same air as her.

As we stand and watch them head down the driveway, a peace falls over me. "I'm putting a gate at the driveway with a security box. You good with that?"

"Yep, just give the guys the code because they should have it."

"Agreed." *And Jack*, I think.

It'll take some finagling to get a buzzer system to the cabin, but sometimes it's nice to have money because I can make just about anything happen. There isn't an amount of money I wouldn't spend to make sure my girl is safe.

I decide to end my day a bit early because I want to soak in the bath with Jenna. It's something I've been dreaming of since I first pictured her here in my cabin. So, after dinner, I lead her to the bathroom and get a hot bath going.

"Relax with me?" I ask.

"Of course, though I thought this would be more of a daytime tub to view the mountains," she says, looking out the black window.

"Just wait," I say as we start stripping out of our clothes. I get in the tub, and then help her in so she can sit with her back to my chest.

I use the remote to turn off the lights in the entire house. Once it's dark, the stars come into view, and they're as clear as day.

"Wow, this is amazing." She gasps when she sees it.

I wrap my arms around her and hold her to me, letting the water soak our muscles. I'm sure she's sore from moving the last few days and tense from dealing with her parents.

"So, I've been thinking," Jenna says.

I tense because my mind goes to the worst-case scenario, but I take a breath and let her talk. "Oh, yeah?" I run my hands over her, calming myself.

"We should put the table in my cabin. It's custom fit for it. Then maybe decorate the house and rent it out. There's a place in town that will manage it, and we can put it up as a vacation rental. We won't have to do anything because the company will take care of everything."

"You know we don't need the money? Are you wanting to hold on to it just in case...?" I can't bring myself to say, *just in case this doesn't work out with us.*

"No, it's not that. It's just the first thing I bought for myself, the first thing I did for myself, and I can't stand the thought of selling it. Not yet, anyway."

"You want to do a vacation rental instead of yearly rentals?"

"Yeah, mostly because the furniture will stay there and it's a great way to advertise your stuff."

Any remaining tension I had is gone. "It's perfect, baby."

We both relax in the bath as our plans fall into place. Everything feels right like this is where we were both meant to end up.

Epilogue

Jenna

I've only been to a handful of funerals in my life. Every one of them has been a social event. When the wealthy die, society sees it as a networking event.

Some go to try to sucker the heirs out of money and property. While some go climbing the social ladder and assume a new standing with the deceased out of the way. Others go just to be seen.

No matter the reason for being there, they all talk like the person who died was this heavenly human with whom they were on a first name basis. We all know it's the furthest thing from the truth, but no one will call anyone on it.

So, when Phoenix said we were going to Cash's brother's funeral, I had no idea what to expect. Mostly because I had no idea what a normal funeral was like, much less what a mountain man's funeral would be like.

The funeral was being held on Cash's land and his brother was being buried there as well. Phoenix spent the last few days working with him to get it all set up.

When we arrive at Cash's place, Emelie and Axel are already there and Emelie rushes over to me. "We're the only girls here, so you aren't allowed to leave my side."

"Who else is here?" I ask.

"Just Bennett, Jack, and the pastor. His brother didn't make friends because he was too paranoid," Emelie says.

Everyone is in black, and Cash stares at the casket sitting next to the grave that Axel, Phoenix, and Bennett dug yesterday. The sermon is short and to the point, and then the guys step up to lower Cash's brother into the ground.

I look at Emelie, and she seems to know what I'm thinking because we both step up on either side of Cash and hold on to his arm. His entire body shudders.

"It's okay, we've got you. You don't have to be strong for any of us, not today," I whisper.

He doesn't reply, but nods as we watch the guys slowly lower the casket into the ground.

It's a very somber and quiet experience. No one talks but the pastor, and it seems even the birds have quieted down.

Once the grave is covered over, we all head to his cabin. Emelie and I lead Cash over to the couch and have him sit down. Axel and Bennett sit with him and Phoenix goes to the kitchen, where Emelie and I join him.

Phoenix is looking through his pantry and fridge. "He has enough food to last him for a while. But he hasn't been in town shopping, much less to the grocery store. All he does is go to the shop, drop off his stuff, and come right back here. His brother handled everything else."

Cash makes the softest fur coats and blankets I've ever seen. They're so much better than anything I've seen my parents' friends wear back in Denver.

"Well, you know we'll help him anyway we can," Emelie says.

We spend the next few hours helping Cash clean up. He wants to get his house back to normal, and that means packing up all the stuff his brother was using. All the medical equipment has to be returned, too.

Emelie and I pitch in to get laundry going and clean up. Thankfully, Cash's place is set up a lot like Axel's in that he uses solar power for the washer and dryer, the fridge, lights, and all that.

Finally, before the sun goes down, we slowly start leaving. Jack and Bennett go first, then Axel and Emelie, leaving Phoenix and me alone with Cash for a few minutes.

"You call us if you need anything. Doesn't matter what. If you need someone to help you in town or have questions, nothing is too small. We'll be happy to come up and help out with anything," I tell him as I give him a hug.

"Thank you." He hugs me a bit tighter before stepping back.

"I'll see you next week at the shop," Cash says to Phoenix.

An unspoken comment that he wants to get back to normal as soon as possible is there, but I can't help but worry.

Where Axel, Phoenix, and Bennett are used to being alone on the mountain, Cash isn't. He never has been because he's always had his brother. Even if his brother was a bit crazy, he never had to face all this alone.

I can leave confident that the mountain men of Whiskey River will rally around him and make sure he's okay. I'm sure of it.

• • • • • • • • • •

A few weeks later I'm sitting on Emelie's couch and having girl time while our guys are out hunting together when the radio starts to make a noise.

"That's odd. The only person who ever calls us on it is Phoenix, and he's out with Axel right now," Emelie says as we get up and we go to the desk where the radio is.

"Emelie, are you there? It's Cash."

We both look at each other before she picks up the radio and answers him. "I'm here, Cash. Is everything okay?"

"Yeah, um, I went to the grocery store today."

His first time at the store. I can only imagine the things that went wrong, and I'm ready to jump into action.

"It was overwhelming, but I, um, I met someone."

I can't help but smile. We might have another girl on Whiskey Mountain before winter after all.

· · · · ●·● · · ·

Get a **bonus Epilogue of Phoenix and Jenna by joining my email!**

Read Cash and Hope's story in **Take Me To The Lake**!

MORE BOOKS BY KACI ROSE

See all of Kaci Rose's Books

Oakside Military Heroes Series

Saving Noah – Lexi and Noah

Saving Easton – Easton and Paisley

Saving Teddy – Teddy and Mia

Saving Levi – Levi and Mandy

Saving Gavin – Gavin and Lauren

Mountain Men of Whiskey River

Take Me To The River – Axel and Emelie

Take Me To The Cabin – Pheonix and Jenna

Take Me To The Lake – Cash and Hope

Take Me To The Mountain – Bennett and Willow

Chasing the Sun Duet

Sunrise – Kade and Lin

Sunset – Jasper and Brynn

Rock Stars of Nashville

She's Still The One – Dallas and Austin

Standalone Books

Texting Titan - Denver and Avery

Accidental Sugar Daddy – Owen and Ellie

Stay With Me Now – David and Ivy

Committed Cowboy – Whiskey Run Cowboys

Stalking His Obsession - Dakota and Grant

Falling In Love on Route 66 – Weston and Rory

Saving Mason - Mason and Paige

Midnight Rose - Ruby and Orlando

Billionaire's Marigold

CONNECT WITH KACI ROSE

Website

Facebook

Kaci Rose Reader's Facebook Group

TikTok

Instagram

Twitter

Goodreads

Book Bub

Join Kaci Rose's VIP List (Newsletter)

About Kaci Rose

Kaci Rose writes steamy contemporary romance mostly set in small towns. She grew up in Florida but longs for the mountains over the beach.

She is a mom to 5 kids and a dog who is scared of his own shadow.

She also writes steamy cowboy romance as Kaci M. Rose.

PLEASE LEAVE A REVIEW!

I love to hear from my readers! Please **head over to your favorite store and leave a review** of what you thought of this book!

Made in United States
North Haven, CT
27 May 2024

52990964R00183